SUTHERLAND'S LAW

LINDSAY GALLOWAY

A PAN ORIGINAL

PAN BOOKS LTD
LONDON AND SYDNEY

First published 1974 by Pan Books Ltd,
Cavaye Place, London SW10 9PG,
by arrangement with the British Broadcasting Corporation

ISBN 0 330 23896 5

Printed in Great Britain by
Richard Clay (The Chaucer Press), Ltd, Bungay, Suffolk

INTRODUCTION

The Procurator Fiscal is a Scottish law officer who has no precise equivalent elsewhere in the civilized world. The nearest is perhaps the District Attorney in the United States, who is also an investigating and prosecuting officer with very wide powers.

The Fiscal is ultimately responsible to the Lord Advocate, who controls the Crown Office, and is charged with the administration of the law in Scotland. The Procurator Fiscal is his local officer and is attached to the Sheriff Court in each district. In the large cities there may be more than one Fiscal attached to the Sheriff Court, and each Fiscal may have one or more Depute Fiscals to assist him. In Glendoran, which is a small town, there is one Procurator Fiscal and one Depute.

All crimes committed in the Sheriffdom (in the case of Glendoran this is an area of about seven thousand square miles) are investigated by the Procurator Fiscal. If the crime is minor the Fiscal will take it before the Sheriff without reference to the Crown Office. In more serious crimes the Fiscal investigates and makes a report to the Crown Office, where the Lord Advocate decides whether or not to prosecute. Certain of these cases will be tried before the Sheriff and a jury. The crimes which the Sheriff is not competent to try are heard in the High Court, when the indictment is prepared by the Crown Office, based on the Fiscal's investigations.

The Fiscal, a civil servant and a member of the Fiscal Service, draws his authority from the Lord Advocate and acts on his behalf. Once evidence of a crime has been laid before him, either by the police or by a private citizen, it is his responsibility to decide whether there is no case to answer, or to initiate further enquiries with a view to presenting a case before the Sheriff or remitting it to the High Court. The Fiscal or his Depute leads the enquiries personally, with the assistance of the police. The decision to proceed with an investigation lies with the Procurator Fiscal alone. At this stage he has wide powers of discretion. There is no on-the-spot supervision. It is assumed that the Fiscal knows his area and what goes on in it; and though he may occasionally make a wrong decision, a Fiscal of standing and repute would almost invariably have the support of the Crown Office and the Lord Advocate.

Although it is the police who attend to the physical investigation of a crime, the Fiscal (and particularly the Fiscal in a semi-rural area like Glendoran, or a Fiscal like John Sutherland with a strong sense of responsibility) is entitled to investigate personally if he so desires. He is entitled, and sometimes obliged, to view the locus of a crime. He interviews witnesses in his office; but he may, if he wishes, go out into the field, so to speak, and see them at their work or in their own homes. He can move around his district and involve himself as deeply as he pleases in the processes of investigation, so long as it serves the purpose of his office, which is the administration of the law and the satisfaction of justice.

He is a qualified solicitor, probably making considerably less money in the Fiscal Service than he would in a private law practice, and he usually joins the Service because of a preference and talent for court work, or out of a sense of vocation. He must be a man of some dedication. He has to make decisions which will irrevocably change the lives of others; he has to live in a community, yet keep himself a little detached; ideally, he should be a man of deep understanding and compassion.

He knows the strengths and the weaknesses of every police officer in his area. He works with them daily, and in many ways is their practical if not their titular head. He knows his Sheriff intimately, and his colleagues, the solicitors and advocates of the district. He is inevitably subject to all sorts of pressures, political, professional and personal, but he must never allow these to touch him or cloud his judgement.

The scope of the Sheriff Court in Scotland – to which the Procurator Fiscal is attached – is extremely wide. The Sheriff can try all criminal cases within his area, except murder, rape, incest and treason. He deals with a great number of civil

6

actions, in which the Procurator Fiscal is seldom involved. In summary cases, sitting alone, the Sheriff may impose three months' imprisonment or a fine of up to £150. Sitting with a jury in solemn procedure, he may impose sentences of up to two years. If he considers a greater punishment desirable, he may remit to the High Court for sentence. He has been described as one of the most powerful judges in the civilized world.

I

Sutherland read the letter twice then laid it on his desk and considered it. He had never thought very highly of Agnew, except as a first class advocate. A rotund, suave man, inclined to be pompous. Yet behind the official phrases there appeared to be a genuine personal concern. He looked up at Christine, waiting patiently at the other side of the desk.

'I take it you've read this?'

'Yes.'

'And what is your opinion, Miss Russell?'

Christine's shoulders moved in a faint shrug under the crisp white blouse. What a clean girl she is, Sutherland thought. He rummaged around for the right word and found it: delectable. If occasionally intransigent.

'Off the record,' he said. 'No need to commit yourself to a profound comment.'

Christine said, 'I agree with him.'

'You agree with him that I'm incapable of conducting the business of this office single-handed?'

'I didn't say that at all. You know I don't think that. And neither does he.'

Sutherland looked at her for a moment in silence. She had warm, dark eyes. When angry, they were warmer and darker. Unusual in a Highland woman. More like the Irish. A touch of Irish blood in her, no doubt, and none the worse for it.

'You implied it, surely.'

'I didn't. I just mean it's been a long, hard winter. And you've been overworked.'

'It keeps the mind occupied.'

'I don't see the point in keeping the mind occupied if it kills you.'

Sutherland smiled. 'I still manage to keep one foot out of the grave.'

'It won't be out of it very long if you go on like this. You've been really bushed once or twice recently. And you've been making . . .' She stopped herself, and shrugged again.

'Mistakes?'

'I was going to say that. But it's not really what I mean.' She hesitated. She had worked for Sutherland for over two years, and there was a good deal of mutual respect. She had a dry sense of humour and was generally outspoken when she felt like it; but at the moment she knew she was on delicate ground. 'It's just that you haven't been making decisions the way you used to,' she said carefully.

Sutherland stared at her in silence. She felt colour coming into her face and it annoyed her.

'I mean, when that woman was knocked down and killed and they tried to blame you for it. You didn't cope with that very well, did you?'

After a moment Sutherland picked up the letter again.

'Mr Agnew suggests one Alexander Duthie as Procurator Fiscal Depute. An Edinburgh degree. Served for a time as a depute in Edinburgh and in Lanarkshire. A Lowlander, would you think? A Sassenach?'

'Possibly.'

Sutherland rose and turned to the big oriel window behind his desk. It was a bright spring day. The bay beyond the roofs of the town was like glass. The island, and the darker hills on the far side of the firth, were sharply etched in the clear air. The sort of day that in his youth had brought a vague sense of excitement. But that was a long time ago.

'You remember Kelso?' he asked over his shoulder.

Kelso had come to Glendoran as Sutherland's depute nine months ago. He was a brisk, impatient young man, and his failure to understand the Highland concept that when God made time he made plenty of it had created some irritation in this Highland town.

Christine said, 'Yes, I remember him,' and waited.

Sutherland was surprised to find himself thinking that poor Kelso had never really had much of a chance in Glendoran. He wondered if he was sometimes inclined to be a little intolerant of Kelso's generation, though he hated intolerance of any kind. When he was almost Kelso's age Sutherland had been well on the way to qualifying in medicine. But the war came along. He went into the army, spent six years in Africa and the Far East, came home and found it difficult to return to medicine, so opted for the law instead. At fifty-two he had acquired a very considerable knowledge of the human animal, but somehow it had not occurred to him that youth and wisdom are infrequent bedfellows. There had been a flaming row, not over a point of law, but because Kelso seemed unaware that compassion is one of the unique privileges of the Fiscal's office. Kelso resigned, and he was not the first of Sutherland's deputes to do so.

'Also,' said Christine, 'I've been remembering what summer's like in Glendoran. Do you?'

Sutherland knew very well what summer in Glendoran was like. Tourists more than trebled the population. The streets became crowded, shopping difficult and disagreeable, parking a car next to impossible. Hotels that had stood empty during the winter, bleak and boarded up against the gales, took on staffs of Greeks, Spaniards and Italians, most of them out to make a quick buck, one or two of them prepared to use disagreeable Latin devices for doing so. Few hippies yet, and, thank God, a negligible drug problem. But the crime rate doubled, and a small but efficient police force was taxed to the limit. Some day the drugs and the hippies would come, possibly this summer. On the island across the bay the sun caught the corrugated iron roof of the boatyard where Sutherland's *Dragon* was still laid up after the winter. There was a good deal of work to be done on her yet, scraping and varnishing, before he could get her into the water again.

'All right,' he said. He turned from the window. 'Draft a letter to Agnew. You know what to say. Tell him that Mr Duthie will be received here with due courtesy. But on a temporary basis – make a point of that. We'll see how it works out.'

Christine said, 'Very good, sir,' a little primly, trying to hide her satisfaction.

Sutherland watched her with a kind of exasperated affection as she gathered up the signed letters from the desk. When she had left the room he turned back to the window. Why, he wondered, was there no longer any promise in a bright spring day? He knew the answer well enough. But he kept it, as he had kept it for five years, at the back of his mind. He stood looking out across the roofs of the town to the bay, where one of the mail boats from the Outer Isles was nudging in to the Railway Pier. Beyond the island, five or six miles across the firth, a drift of smoke rose from the shoulder of a hill. Late in the year for heather burning, he thought. Not on Willie McWhirter's ground. Willie's moors were always well advanced. Sooner or later he would get Willie's invitation to shoot some grouse on the Twelfth. Sutherland discovered that it was a prospect that no longer appealed to him. This year he would dream up some prior engagement.

A family of grouse exploded out of the heather as McWhirter and his head keeper, McGuffie, came over a rise in the ground.

McWhirter stopped to watch them as they beat low across the moor. He was a vigorous man, approaching fifty. Even in old tweeds he had the casually-groomed look that generally comes with much money. His boyhood had passed in a large red sandstone villa in a well-to-do district on the south side of Glasgow's river, never far from the sound of the riveters' hammers and the river traffic. When the time came he went into the shipping industry, and in his prime years was thrusting, arrogant and ruthless until he had made a couple of million or so, when he mellowed slightly.

McGuffie considered him to be a satisfactory employer. He paid a fair wage, knew what he wanted, and had the money to maintain a sporting estate in a way few people did these days. McGuffie was a lean, dark man from Wester Ross with a satiric sense of humour and the Highlander's total lack of servility.

After the grouse had dipped out of sight, McWhirter said: 'You've done well, McGuffie. The moor's in very good shape this year.'

McGuffie was complacently aware of this. Much work had gone into it. The small areas of burnt heather had been judiciously selected. There was plenty of old heather to give shelter, plenty of grit down, few vermin. But he was prepared to acknowledge a certain amount of assistance from above.

'The weather's helped us. It'll bring on the new growth now and give the young birds a chance.'

'How many guns will it take?'

'How many days will you be wanting, laird?'

'Five days from the Twelfth. Maybe a couple of days later in the month. I know it's looking a long way ahead.'

McGuffie considered for a moment.

'It should provide good sport for a dozen guns.'

'Good.'

McWhirter turned away and resumed walking, drawing deep breaths of his own fresh air. McGuffie walked two or three yards behind him.

Presently the ground began to fall away in front of them, opening up a vista of bright water and beyond it the mainland with its backdrop of mountains, still with patches of snow in the high gullies.

McWhirter stopped again, suddenly, and stood for a moment staring down the hill in front of him.

'What the devil is that, McGuffie?'

McGuffie drew alongside him and stopped.

'It's a wee house, laird,' he said.

It was some distance below them in a hollow, about two hundred yards away, a small house built of logs with a shingle roof. Crisp turf, patches of gorse and one or two small outcrops of rock made a pleasant, naturally landscaped setting.

McWhirter said: 'On my land?'

'It's just over the march, on the McAllister side,' said McGuffie.

'What's McAllister playing at? Building holiday cottages? Cashing in?'

McGuffie shrugged. 'I wouldn't know, laird.'

'Well, I can't have this going on, whatever it is.' He began to walk briskly down through the heather, towards the house.

Angus McInnes sat in front of the small house he had built with

13

his own two hands, shaping a piece of wood. He worked with the leisureliness of complete content, enjoying the feel of the wood, the warmth of the mild May sun and the sound of the birds, which had now become accustomed to him and paid him the compliment of ignoring his presence, except when he put out the food for them. He was eighty years old; he had worked for a living with his hands for most of that time, and all the skill they had acquired had gone into the making of the house. It was almost finished. Only a few details remained, and he was pleased with it. Not a nailhead showed, inside or out. Not a joint, in doors or windows or under the wide eaves, would let in the slightest whisper of the winter gales. He had worked to no plan. The whole thing had come out of his head. But the shape, now it had taken solid form, gave him pleasure. It seemed to grow out of the land. Already the hollow had taken on a feeling of home. The old dog had established his daytime place under a thicket of gorse. The skep of bees under the wind-twisted mountain ash was active. A man could be content here to let the last years come and go.

He was a broad, strong old man, not above average height, with a weathered face. His wind-washed blue eyes could see a sheep with a shoulder out, on the face of a mountain, when a townsman would see only the mountain. When he had finished with the piece of wood he laid it aside and sat for a moment contemplating his view. The ground in front dipped down for a hundred yards to a small bay with an island in it, making a good anchorage if ever he felt inclined to get a boat and put out a few lobster pots. The bay opened out into the firth, and beyond that, beyond the mainland shore, the mountains were dominated by the harsh, dark peak of the Bruaich. The Bruaich had another name to it, but he could not remember it for the moment. He heard the distant thump of diesel engines, and after a moment or two a pair of fishing boats appeared round the shoulder of land to the south, making across the firth to Glendoran. They were low in the water, on the way home after a night's fishing off the East Shore. He recognized one of them as *The Maid of Lorne*. James Campbell had brought her into Carrapool once or twice in the old days, when bad weather had caught him out. A man not unlike himself; but a good twenty years younger, of course.

The collie stirred under the gorse thicket, lifted its head and growled. McInnes rose after a moment and walked to the gable end of the house. His movements were deliberate, as though he knew he had all the time in the world, or that time was of no consequence. He looked up the hill and saw two men at the march fence. The collie was at his side now, growling deep in its throat.

'*Laigh sios, Linn!*' McInnes said softly, and waited.

McWhirter had stopped at the wire fence marking the end of his land and was frowning down at the house.

'It's on the McAllister side, anyhow,' he said, a little irritably. If it had been on his own side the matter would have been simple.

McGuffie said, 'I don't think it's on McAllister's land, all the same. I seem to remember he sold a strip of it, just two or three acres, to an old fellow called McInnes.'

McWhirter looked round at him and said sharply: 'Why didn't I know about this?'

McGuffie shrugged. 'It would be about twenty years ago, laird. Before you came to Glengarve. And there's been neither sight nor sound of McInnes until now.'

'What the devil was McAllister thinking about? Selling a piece of land like this.'

'I suppose he would be feeling it was of no particular value to him. He's got fifteen hundred acres of hill grazing anyhow.'

'Didn't he realize what he was doing? We'll have this sort of thing growing all over the place like a crop of mushrooms.'

He gestured and McGuffie heaved up the top strand of the barbed wire fence so that McWhirter could ease himself through.

Angus McInnes watched the two men as they came down the hill towards him. When they were near enough he called out a greeting.

'*Latha math dhuibh a dhaoine uaisle!*'

McGuffie said, '*Latha math dhuit fhein.*'

McWhirter nodded briefly and walked past Angus, round to the front of the house.

McGuffie said, 'That is Sir William McWhirter of Glengarve,' and somehow managed to make it sound like an apology.

They followed McWhirter, who looked round at Angus as they approached.

'What's going on here?' he asked. His manner was peremptory. Angus gave him a speculative look and turned to McGuffie.

'*Abair ris an duine uasal nach'eil beurla agam,*' he said, gently.

McGuffie translated in a carefully neutral voice. 'He says he doesn't speak English, laird.'

McWhirter gave Angus a cold stare. 'I find that hard to believe. We're not in the eighteenth century, you know.'

Angus spoke again in the Gaelic, and McGuffie said, 'He's been crofting all his life in a part of Morven where they have no need of the English.'

'Then what's he doing here?'

'*De tha thu a deanamh an so mata?*' McGuffie asked, and Angus replied at some length, his voice still gentle. When he had finished, McGuffie looked round at McWhirter. 'He says he is Angus McInnes. That he bought this small piece of land to build a house on when the time came. Now that his wife is dead and his children scattered about the world, he wants nothing but to end his days here in peace.'

McWhirter made an indeterminate noise. He could see no reason to disbelieve the story, and this irritated him. He turned back to the house. It was a pretty enough place, certainly no eyesore, and seemed well enough put together. Not much health hazard in a remote corner like this. Anyhow, McInnes had doubtless never known anything better than an earth closet and appeared to have survived remarkably well on it.

'Has he got planning permission?' he asked suddenly. 'If there was a building warrant I should have been consulted. Adjacent property.'

McGuffie said, '*An d'fhuair the cead tigh a thogail?*'

Angus stared at him in astonishment and said, in the Gaelic, 'Why would I be needing permission to build a house on my own land?'

'Tell him no one can build a house nowadays without permission,' McWhirter said, a little impatiently, 'on his own land or anywhere else.'

McGuffie did so. Angus took out an old short-stemmed pipe and began to cut neat slices of black tobacco from a plug. When he had cut sufficient he put the plug away and began to grind the cut tobacco in the palm of his hand. McWhirter moved restlessly.

'Well? Did he understand?'

'Yes, yes, he understood all right,' said McGuffie, soothingly. 'As far as it's possible to understand why we have to get permission to do just about anything these days. He'll just be giving it a little thought.'

Angus put a match to his pipe. His pale eyes roamed over the firth below, where a brisk breeze was plucking the spray from the tops of the white horses.

'*De th'aige ri dheanamh ris-san co dhiu tha cead agam no nach'eil?*' he asked, turning back to McGuffie.

McGuffie rubbed his nose gently with his thumb, as much as anything to cover his mouth, which was beginning to twitch a little.

'He's asking, laird, what it's got to do with you whether he has permission or not.'

McWhirter said sharply: 'Tell him I'm a Justice of the Peace, McGuffie. I like to see the Law treated with a certain amount of respect.'

Angus said in the Gaelic, with a rising note of indignation in his voice: 'Tell the gentleman I will build a house on my own land if I want to. Tell him I will die in it if I want to. And no one will stop me.'

McGuffie translated and McWhirter said angrily, 'We'll see about that.'

Angus removed his pipe and spat carefully into the heather a couple of feet from one of the shoes that Lobb had made for McWhirter with loving care. '*Rachadh e fhein 's a lagh do theinntean dearg infrinn airson mile bliadhna,*' he said angrily. '*Cha chuir sin dragh orm-sa.*'

McGuffie looked uneasy.

McWhirter said, 'Well?'

'He's a bit angry,' said McGuffie.

'So am I. What did he say?'

McGuffie hesitated. 'Well, in a kind of a free translation, laird, he says that you can take your law and go and sit with it on the hot hob of hell for a thousand years, so far as he is concerned.'

McWhirter stared furiously at Angus for a moment, then turned on his heel and walked away.

McGuffie grinned at Angus. 'You've done it now,' he said cheerfully and turned to follow McWhirter.

Angus watched them as they climbed the hill towards the march, and after a moment he called after them, '*Airson da mhile bliadhna!*'

Then his eye fell on the old twelve-bore gun propped against the wall near the door of the house.

'For two thousand years, laird, he says,' McGuffie remarked as he raised the top strand of the fence. McWhirter gave him a bleak look and began to ease himself through the gap.

The first of the gunshots rang out close behind them. McWhirter threw himself into the heather on the far side of the fence. McGuffie scrambled through without dignity as the second shot rang out and threw himself down beside his employer. Grouse chattered and took to the air nearby. The echoes of the shots died away across the moor and there was silence except for the breeze moaning faintly in the wires of the fence.

After a moment McGuffie raised himself cautiously on one elbow and looked at the back of his employer's head, which was all he could see of it, buried deep among the heather stems.

'Did he get you, laird?' he enquired, anxiously.

II

The Sheriff Court at Glendoran had tall windows along two sides letting in plenty of light and a good deal of traffic noise. At times, when the fish lorries were rumbling south from the harbour, speech became impossible and the Court lapsed into a moody silence until the rumbling had died away and the Sheriff said, 'Yes, Mr Sutherland. You were saying?'

The bench was separated from the rest of the courtroom by a three foot high wall-to-wall mahogany partition. The Sheriff sat behind this under a coat of arms. Below him, on the other side of the partition, the Sheriff Clerk sat at a large square table with the advocates and the Fiscal. Beyond the table was the dock, and beyond that the public benches. Below the Sheriff, on his left, were the jury benches, and on his right the witness box. The old wood and the linoleum on the floors had acquired a mellow glow through the passing of the years and the industry of Cairns, the court usher. The place smelled faintly of wax polish and disinfectant.

The bench was generally occupied by Sheriff Archibald Derwent. He was a man of about sixty, a little gaunt, with direct, penetrating eyes and a resonant voice which he used effectively. His occasional outbursts of judicial wit had inevitably lost some of their originality for the regulars but still went down well with the public and the press. Sutherland considered him to be a good sheriff, conscious of his responsibilities as a judge with very wide powers, if sometimes irritable and impatient on days when the weather was fine and the golf course in good playing condition.

A pale, nervous girl sat in the dock. She was bewildered by her surroundings, the hushed court, the muted sounds from the public benches behind her; bewildered by what she had done and by what had happened to her; and she was very frightened of the man in the black gown and short wig with the white fall at his throat who sat on the bench above her, frowning as he leafed through the notes he had written assiduously throughout her trial.

Presently he looked up from the notes, stared down at her for a moment, and said, 'Annie Gillies, you have been guilty of a very serious offence.'

'Stand up when his Lordship speaks to you,' the Sheriff Clerk said.

The girl said, 'Yes, sir,' and blushed. Glendoran had the unusual distinction of a Sheriff Clerk with raven black hair, a pleasant contralto voice and, at less solemn moments, an engaging smile. Annie Gillies stood up and the Sheriff continued.

'It is an offence for which the Law prescribes a heavy punishment. You subjected the parents of the child you took away to extreme anguish. You seem to have taken reasonable care of it – of this there seems to be some evidence, to which the Procurator Fiscal has properly drawn the attention of the Court. But the parents were not to know that you were doing so, and it could not relieve their mental suffering at the time. For five days the police wasted a good deal of energy, time and public money looking for you . . .'

Sutherland drew his gown about him and settled well back in his chair, staring up at the light fixture, like a large white goldfish bowl, high above the well of the court. It was a posture which could suggest either profound concentration or boredom. He was aware that Archie Derwent had never quite been able to decide which, and that it occasionally brought him a little more quickly to the point.

After a moment or two the Sheriff stopped, gave Sutherland a brief glance, referred to his notes again and looked back at the girl in the dock.

'However,' he said, 'the report of the psychiatrist who examined you while you were awaiting trial confirms my view that imprisonment would not be appropriate in your case. I am therefore going to place you on probation for two years. The Probation Officer will see you before you leave the court.'

The girl gave a small gasp of surprise and relief and whispered, 'Thank you, sir.'

The Sheriff closed his notebook, sat back and looked up at the goldfish bowl.

There was movement in the court. One or two people rose and shuffled out of the public benches. A woman police constable opened the door of the dock and beckoned to Annie Gillies. Cairns, the court usher, went out through the swing doors and his voice could be heard calling in the distance, 'Thomas McAlpine! Thomas McAlpine!'

Sutherland said, 'Thomas McAlpine?' and began to rummage through the papers on the table in front of him.

'Breach of the peace,' said the Sheriff Clerk.

Sutherland frowned and said, 'Again?'

The Sheriff Clerk smiled. 'I'm afraid so.'

A small square man in a shabby blue suit came in through the swing doors followed by two young constables. He was unshaven and had no tie on but he walked bow-legged with the confidence and familiarity of a professional footballer coming out for a game on his home ground. He let himself into the dock, closed the door carefully and smiled affably at Sutherland and the Sheriff Clerk. The Sheriff lowered his gaze from the goldfish bowl and leant forward.

'You are going to leave a yawning void in all our lives, McAlpine, if you ever forego strong liquor.'

McAlpine grinned. 'I'm sure I wouldnae want to do that, m'lud.'

'I'm sure you wouldn't . . . Yes, Mr Sutherland.'

Sutherland rose to his feet and said, 'Constable Keith.'

One of the young constables stepped up into the witness box.

Alexander Duthie arrived at Glendoran in a small sports car nosing through the morning traffic of the main street like an angry wasp. Where the street opened out, with shops and hotels on the one hand and the curve of the bay on the other, Duthie pulled in to the side and parked. He got out, crossed to the sea wall and surveyed his surroundings.

It was a crisp, spring morning. The tide was well in. Small pleasure craft bobbed at their moorings. At the South Pier one of the mail steamers was disembarking passengers, livestock, cars and lorries from the Outer Isles. Over to the left at the fish quay, the fishing boats were in, lying two or three abreast, unloading the night's catch. Glendoran had not yet been taken over by the summer tourists and still belonged to the indigenous inhabitants. To Duthie, most of them seemed to be tall men in plus-fours and deerstalkers with nailed shoes that clattered confidently on the pavements, and handsome women with clear skins in serviceable tweeds and brogues. The voices were soft and cheerful without the broad, harsh accents of the Lowland towns. Now and again he caught a snatch of the Gaelic, spoken as a native tongue. The place had a good, pungent smell about it; a mixture of sea water, tarred rope, fish, a whiff of diesel oil. But there was something else under-lying it. Perhaps the scent of tangled seaweed on deserted beaches far beyond the bay. Once in the Indian Ocean a hundred miles from any land he had caught the scent of spices on the warm breeze. This had the same feeling, subtle and promising.

It was not Duthie's scene. But he had to admit to himself that it was fresh, lively and a pleasant change. He was attracted by the bustle on the fish quay and began to walk round the sea wall towards it.

The fish quay was lined on one side by the small wooden shacks of the fish buyers and company agents, and on the other by the masts and derricks of the boats. Between was confusion. Lorries stacked with fish boxes dripping melting ice. Large men with walnut brown faces in bright yellow oilskins standing about in groups, arguing cheerfully about the catch, the weather, the prospects for tonight. Fish buyers in tight Burton suits inspecting samples and disputing prices. At the quay's edge, boats' derricks lowering big baskets into the holds and hoisting them again to tip masses of bright, slithering herring already gutted into the fish boxes stacked high on the lorries drawn up alongside. Old men carrying plastic bags scavenging for fish that had dropped from the baskets on to the quay, selecting and rejecting like discriminating housewives. Down on the decks of the boats, hands swabbing away the night's fish scales with gushing hoses; great neat piles of nets and coils of ropes and wire hawsers; brightly coloured dahn buoys and markers piled in the sterns.

Underfoot the quay was crossed with a maze of mooring lines, littered with fish heads and other garbage which would not be cleared until the boats had sailed again. Slippery with patches of melted ice and wet planking. The air was filled with the clatter of the donkey engines, the rasp and creak of the derricks, and the screaming of the big herring gulls circling endlessly, low overhead, diving to fight and squabble over scraps of fish offal. They perched on mastheads, on bollards, on empty fish boxes, and stared with bright indignant eyes, for they were the original inhabitants. They had been here long before Glendoran was a town.

Two men came out of the Seamen's Mission at the far end of the quay and walked towards the boats. Hugh McPhail was a lean, dark man of about thirty in seaboots and an oilskin jacket. He was saved from being handsome by eyes set a little too close together. Ian Campbell, also in seaboots and an oilskin, was more solidly built and two or three years older. A ruddy faced, jovial man, but with no great liking for his companion. As they came near the edge of the quay McPhail stopped to light a cigarette, taking his time about it.

Ian said, 'Keep moving, Hughie. The weather's not going to wait for us,' and he put a big hand between McPhail's shoulderblades and pushed. McPhail half turned, caught his foot on a mooring line and went down on his hands and knees at the edge of the quay.

Ian grinned, swung a leg over the side of the quay and went down an iron ladder to the deck of *The Maid of Lorne* a dozen feet below. McPhail crouched where he was, watching the grinning face disappear below the level of the quay, and said nothing.

The Maid of Lorne was eighty feet long and eighteen feet in the beam. She was one of the older boats, wooden built, but James Campbell, her skipper, saw to it that she was well cared for. Her varnish and paintwork were fresh, her deck machinery was clean and well greased, her nets, ropes and warps were sound and neatly stowed. He was leaning out of the side window of the wheelhouse as his eldest son went aft along the waist.

23

'That was a daft thing to do, Ian,' he said. 'You might have broken his neck.'

Ian looked up at him and said, 'No such luck,' without heat. He went on past the wheelhouse to the companion hatch giving access to the living quarters. The skipper turned his head and watched McPhail coming down the ladder to the deck. No such luck, he thought. Ian's right. It would be the easy way out.

William Campbell, the skipper's younger son, seventeen years old, was hosing the forward deck as McPhail came down from the quay. He turned the hose over the side for a moment and called to McPhail, 'Are you okay, Hughie?'

McPhail gave him a tight smile and said, 'I'm okay, boy. I just tripped. Nothing to make a fuss about.' He turned away and walked aft. The boy watched him with a worried frown on his face, then he brought the hose inboard again and went on with his work.

Two men in oilskins were standing beside a fish lorry a little way along the quay, looking down at *The Maid of Lorne*. One of them took his pipe from his mouth.

'Some dark night,' he said, 'that fellow's going to fall over the side.'

Duthie, who was standing nearby, found the remark interesting.

'Which fellow?' he asked.

The man turned and looked at him carefully, at the city suit, the polished shoes, at the intelligent face with the slightly beaten-up look and a quirk of humour at the mouth, and said, 'Are you looking for somebody?'

Duthie said, 'The Sheriff Court.'

'Ay, well, you'll no find it on the fish quay,' the man said. 'It's back in the town there. Off the main square.'

Duthie said, 'Thanks,' and turned away. The brush-off, the closed community suspicious of outsiders, were a familiar part of his life. He walked back along the quay towards his car.

Duthie found a space outside the Sheriff Court building and eased his car into it. He gunned the engine a couple of times, got out and slammed the door. He looked up with some distaste at the grey, bleak granite façade, and went inside.

Upstairs in the courtroom, Sheriff Derwent said, 'Close the windows, usher. If we are to have the option of not hearing the Fiscal's remarks, or of being asphyxiated, duty compels us to choose the latter.'

He was rewarded with an indulgent smile from Sutherland and a titter from the public benches.

'Yes, Mr Sutherland?' he said, and leant back and stared up at the goldfish bowl.

Duthie found himself in a large gloomy entrance hall. Up to shoulder height the walls were painted bile green and above that a dark canary yellow. A wide stone staircase led upwards from the back of the hall to where he presumed the courtroom to be. He could hear the murmur of voices from above. There were several mahogany doors, dark and sombre like the rest of the place. One of these was marked in faded gold letters, PROCURATOR FISCAL'S OFFICE. Duthie knocked politely on it and went through.

Christine heard the door but continued typing for a moment before looking up. When she did so, Duthie was leaning on the counter watching her through the hatch in the frosted glass partition with obvious approval. The years in her father's manse, after her mother had died, had given her a sort of poise and coolness, a sort of primness which was not really part of her character, but she found it useful at times.

'Yes?' she said, and managed to make the word tinkle like a piece of ice in a dry martini.

Duthie straightened up. 'Mr Sutherland,' he said. 'The Procurator Fiscal.'

Christine said: 'He's in court. Can I help you?'

Duthie gave her a friendly smile. 'My name's Duthie. Alexander for short.'

'Oh, yes, Mr Duthie. You'd better come in.' She rose and opened the door at the end of the partition separating the small waiting area from the main office. 'We've been expecting you,' she said, as Duthie came through. 'For some time.'

Duthie grinned. 'I know. I'm late. I'd some things to clear up before I left. You know how it is.'

Christine said, 'I don't expect the Court will rise for another half hour. Would you like some tea?'

'If you're making it.'

'I'm always making it. The police force seems to think this is a sort of tea bar. And the Fiscal's capacity is remarkable.'

'I've been hearing quite a lot about him,' Duthie said.

She gave him a cool, direct stare. 'Have you?'

'What's he like? Or is that a silly question?'

'Yes, it is. Anyhow, you'll find out for yourself. If you survive.'

Duthie grinned again. Christine went into a large cupboard where stationery and files were stored and the tea was made. Cups clattered. Duthie inspected the room. It was large and well-lit with unexpected touches – two or three good water-colours and a vase of daffodils. Bookshelves and filing cabinets and a big desk in the middle of the room with the papers on it arranged neatly. There were a couple of easy chairs. It was all clean, polished and fresh. This girl was competent, Duthie thought, as well as decorative. An unusual combination.

There were two doors at the far end of the room, one of them standing half open. Duthie went over to it and looked inside. He found a large bare room with sombre walls and strictly functional furnishings: three metal chairs with plastic seats against one wall, a bookcase filled with old leather-bound books against another, a flat-topped desk with a plain swivel chair behind it and a bentwood coat rack. He crossed to the window. It looked down on a courtyard where a young constable in shirtsleeves was polishing a police car. The window was slightly open at the top and he could hear the man whistling cheerfully under his breath, as though he were grooming a horse.

From the door Christine said, 'How clever of you to guess! This *is* your room.'

Duthie turned. 'It's a cosy little nest, isn't it?'

She smiled. 'It won't tempt you to linger after office hours, anyhow.'

'Don't be too sure,' Duthie said. 'I'm an enthusiast.'

He ran his eye along the bookshelves.

'Where on earth did these come from?'

Christine shrugged. 'They've always been here.'

'Left by the Romans, I expect,' Duthie said. 'I didn't know they got as far north.'

Duthie followed the girl out into the main office, where they drank tea: Woolworth mugs and Georgian silver sugar bowl and milk jug. He found himself becoming increasingly interested in Sutherland.

'Is he married?' he asked.

The girl said, 'Not now. His wife died five years ago.'

He decided not to enquire into the circumstances of her death. This girl was not exactly antagonistic, but she was making it quite clear that he was a newcomer, not yet to be trusted. He decided to go up and watch Sutherland at work in the court.

He was too late. The court was rising when he got there. The Sheriff, exchanging bows with the Fiscal and a solicitor, walked to a door behind the mahogany partition and disappeared into his private room. The usher followed, carrying his notebooks. Derwent was a meticulous man and liked to make copious notes. Duthie waited until the court had cleared a little. Sutherland was shuffling his papers together when Duthie spoke behind him.

'Mr Sutherland?'

Sutherland straightened up and turned, and Duthie, who was above average height, was surprised to find himself looking up at a man considerably larger than himself. He was also surprised at the glint of humour in the eyes that inspected him carefully before Sutherland replied. As he had told the girl, he had heard quite a lot about Sutherland, of his impatience and truculence, of a tongue that could cut like a stock-whip. Only one or two had hinted that the experience of working with him might be rewarding.

'Mr Duthie, I presume?' Sutherland said, when he had seen all he wanted.

'Yes. I'm sorry I'm late, sir.'

'Better late than never, I suppose,' Sutherland said. 'This is Miss Hamilton, who is – happily for all of us – our Sheriff Clerk. And this is Mr Pringle, one of the more illustrious members of our local Bar.'

Liz Hamilton gave Duthie a friendly smile. Pringle, a large, shapeless man in a shabby blue suit and black gown, nodded briefly and Duthie took an instant and unreasonable dislike for him.

Sutherland said, 'I'm sorry you couldn't make it a little earlier. I have to be in Edinburgh for a couple of days. I'd like to have shown you the ropes.'

Liz Hamilton said, 'Our Fiscal believes in throwing his deputes in at the deep end. But I'm sure you'll be all right, Mr Duthie. I don't think there's anything of importance coming up.'

Duthie grinned and said, 'I appreciate your confidence in me.'

Sutherland gathered up his papers. 'Come along,' he said. 'At least I can show you the geography.'

He led the way out through the swing doors. As they were crossing the landing the Sheriff came out of his room and Sutherland stopped.

'I'd like you to meet Mr Duthie, Sheriff. My new depute.'

'How do you do, Mr Duthie,' said the Sheriff, as they shook hands, and added agreeably, 'I wonder how long you're going to last. Did you apply for this position?'

Duthie said, 'No, sir. I was invited to apply.'

'Are you a country man?' the Sheriff asked.

Duthie said, 'No, sir. I've been a depute in Edinburgh and in one of the Lanarkshire towns for the past couple of years.'

The Sheriff said, 'You prefer the rough and tumble?'

'Definitely.'

'You won't be entirely deprived of it here, I assure you.'

Duthie said, 'It'll be quieter, though.'

'It'll be different, Mr Duthie,' the Sheriff said. 'It'll be different.'

He walked downstairs with them.

Pringle came down shortly afterwards and crossed the street to the County Buildings, where he had a brief meeting with George Campbell, the County Clerk, a tall, lean, earnest, careful man, soberly dressed and convinced that he carried an almost insupportable burden of responsibility. He was careful now about the information Pringle gave him.

'The correct procedure,' he said, 'would be for me to write to the man, reminding him that planning permission has to be obtained. I would enclose a Form D1, and if he completes this I have no doubt that my Planning Committee would grant consent, retrospectively, so to speak. Unless, of course, the building has defects from a planning point of view. Then he would be invited to put these right.'

Pringle said, 'Supposing he doesn't oblige? I mean, by completing the form – what is it? – D1?'

'I don't imagine he would be so foolish.'

'Not foolish, perhaps,' said Pringle. 'There's nothing else you can do?'

'Nothing,' said Campbell. 'At the moment.'

Pringle rose. 'We'll leave it at that, then. No doubt you'll keep me advised.'

'Yes, yes, of course, Mr Pringle,' said Campbell, and saw his visitor to the door.

It was three days before the letter reached Angus McInnes. He put it unopened under a disused tea-caddy on the mantelpiece, where it could lie until the mood was on him to deal with it.

Sutherland stood with a mug of tea in one hand in front of a large contoured wall map in his office.

'We cover a very large area, Duthie,' he said, and looked round. 'Have you another name, by the way?'

Duthie said, 'Alexander. I'll settle for Alec.'

'I'm obliged to you.' Sutherland turned back to the map. 'Some very inaccessible country here. You'd be surprised what can happen in the remoter parts. There's a big power scheme back there, for instance. Gives a lot of trouble. Three thousand men working on it. Living in construction camps. Most of them Poles, Italians or Irish, and not on the whole the best representatives of their race.'

Duthie asked, 'What about the town itself?'

'Population in winter about ten thousand. Problems mainly domestic but sometimes messy. Some of the local boys can get quite tough with a dram inside them.'

'An incest belt with a Gaelic mafia,' Duthie said, before he could stop himself.

Sutherland gave him a brief glance. 'I wouldn't call it that in public, if I were you.' He turned away from the map. 'In summer we have a population explosion. Tourists from all over the world. We get remarkably cosmopolitan. It's reflected in the crime statistics.'

Duthie looked round the room. It had a comfortable lived-in feeling: good furniture, more water-colours from the same brush, fishing rods and golf clubs in one corner, the big oriel commanding the harbour.

'You've got a better nest than I have,' he said.

Sutherland smiled and said, 'I've been feathering it for some years.'

'What are the police like?' Duthie asked.

'Like everywhere else. They have their little ways. Sergeant McKechnie will be helpful. Knows the idiosyncracies of almost everyone in the county. He may seem a little slow to you. But you'll recall the Spaniard, touring in the Highlands, who asked for a translation of mañana?'

'No.'

'He was told there was no word in the Gaelic that conveyed the same sense of urgency.' Sutherland looked at his watch. 'Time I was away. You'll find that the office runs itself. Miss Russell may give the appearance of being a little proper. But she knows – don't misunderstand me – she knows her onions.'

He picked up his briefcase and went through to the main office. Christine looked up from her desk.

'Two in custody,' she said. 'Breach of the peace. The sergeant would like to know what you want done with them.'

'Local boys?' Sutherland asked.

'Old friends.'

'He can turn them loose for tonight. Mr Duthie will deal with them in the morning. I'm sure he can handle this sort of thing very competently, with his experience of urban crime.'

He gave Duthie a paternal look that removed a little of the sting, and went out. Duthie looked round at Christine. She gave him a friendly smile.

'Well,' she said, 'you're the boss.'

Duthie decided that he would ask her to spend the evening showing him the town.

III

James Campbell, who was in no way related to the County Clerk, was alone in the wheelhouse of *The Maid of Lorne*. It was dusk. The islands a mile or two off on the port side were sharp silhouettes against the brilliant, flaming backcloth of the dying sunset. Over to the east the sky and the sea were black. The lights of *The Good Intent* were bright, about half a mile away on the starboard beam. Beyond her, six or eight miles off, the Garbh Sgeir light flashed intermittently. There was a heavy ground swell and the deck heaved under James's feet, but it was peaceful in the wheelhouse. The big diesel rumbled a couple of decks below. The echo-sounder pinged rhythmically. The green radar screen flickered. Garbled voices from other boats in the area sounded occasionally on the RT. Below on the forward deck the boy Willie was sorting out some gear under the glaring worklights.

James let his mind wander back, as he was inclined to do lately, to the days when the herring were still in Loch Fyne and he was fishing out of a Kintyre village. The boats were smaller but the inshore waters were kinder and there was none of this long haul to the fishing grounds. He could be sure of spending most nights at home, with a compact and loving family. But the herring had moved away to more distant waters, for no particular reason that anyone knew of. Strangers had married into the family. It was no longer compact, and at times it was far from loving, held together by little more than an old loyalty.

The rhythm of the echo-sounder changed slightly as it began to find fish. They would be into the fishing grounds soon, and into the area where the wrecks lay. James knew the position of most of them precisely. There were the merchantmen and a destroyer from the first World War, and two submarines and a floating dock from the second; and there was the freighter with the cargo of whisky which obligingly ran herself on to a submerged reef in 1942 and provided generously for the islanders throughout the lean years that followed. Now and again a bottle of it might still be produced with great ceremony at the end of a convivial evening. But there were other wrecks, uncharted, which could turn out to be no cause for celebration. They could foul five hundred pounds' worth of net and tear it to pieces.

The men were on deck now in their bright yellow oilskins getting the gear ready for the first shot of the night. The boy Willie came up into the wheelhouse and James gave him the wheel.

'Just try and keep her head the way she is,' he said. 'She's inclined to jump about a bit in this sea.'

She'll jump about a bit more, he thought, before the night's out. The wind was freshening, backing round to the north west. They would have a rough passage home to Glendoran in the morning. He opened the window on the starboard side and leant out. *The Good Intent* was two or three hundred yards away and a little astern of them. He waited until she was in position, then gave the word and the trawl was shot. He watched it streaming out in a wide arc, visible in the worklights of the two boats. Then he watched the wire warps running out, through fairleads and rollers along the starboard side, over the block on the gallows on the quarter. He frowned and turned to look out of the front window over the forward deck, to where Hugh McPhail was working the winch.

'He's letting them run out too fast,' he said. 'A wee touch less throttle, Willie.'

Willie eased the throttle back and the rumble of the diesel under their feet fell away slightly. James watched McPhail uneasily. He saw Ian going forward, stepping over the boards of the fish pounds in his heavy thigh boots, and heard his angry shout above the rattle of the winch.

'For God's sake, Hughie! Are you an engineer or a garage mechanic? Can you no handle a winch yet?'

As Ian came forward McPhail said, 'What's the matter with you?'

'You're letting the warps out too fast! They'll get fouled in the gallows.'

McPhail grinned and said, 'Ach, away with you! They're going out fine.'

Ian shouted, 'You bloody idiot! You haven't got a train to catch!'

He tried to push McPhail aside. McPhail's narrow face darkened with anger and he clung to the controls of the winch. The whine and clatter of the winch increased suddenly. The steel wires screeched in the fairleads. Ian took a step back, measured the distance and swung at McPhail. McPhail spun round as he took the blow on the shoulder. He fetched up on his hands and knees in the scuppers with only the low gunwale, less than waist high, between him and the white water foaming along the boat's side.

In the wheelhouse, James turned.

'Just keep her head the way she is, Willie,' he said, and went down the wheelhouse ladder with remarkable agility for a man of his years.

Duthie and Christine had a leisurely and reasonably satisfactory dinner in an establishment known as The Station Hotel. It was built when Glendoran became a railhead and still had a kind of faded Victorian majesty. It had been an overnight stopping place for peers and cabinet ministers and the upper crust generally for almost a hundred years, as they travelled to or from Highland shooting lodges and sporting estates. Thick carpets that had felt the footfalls of the hereditary rich had worn thin in places and the gilded cornices were dull and dusty. Long dead stags stared down with detached disapproval, as they collected cobwebs, at today's tourists moving through the gloomy halls and corridors. But tradition lingered. Highland hospitality, good solid food, and no foreign servants. It delighted Duthie.

During the meal, aware that Christine had steered him delicately away from herself, Duthie talked about his own

33

background. Born in Hawick, in the Border Country, in 1942. Son of a long line of Border solicitors. Educated Hawick and Edinburgh University, where he took an Honours degree in Law. The residue from an aunt's estate gave him limited private means and allowed him to throw up a share in a lucrative law practice and enter the Fiscal Service. His family had found this incomprehensible. So did Christine.

'I was interested in crime,' Duthie said. 'I suppose everybody is. But I found Havelock Ellis in my father's library when I was nine. I couldn't put it down, as they say.'

'Crime!' she said, scathingly. 'Poaching? Shoplifting? Baby bashing? Drunks brawling outside a pub? That's about all you see in this business, most of the time. Routine stuff. D'you like routine?'

'No. I should really have gone into the police. Got into the CID. I might do that yet.'

After a little she asked, 'Engaged?'

'Twice,' he said. 'But they both got away.'

Afterwards they walked round the town. It was a blustery but quite mild evening. They dropped in to one or two of the pubs, which Duthie found dull though no doubt they would brighten up when the tourist season got under way. He liked one of them: a small place in a back street near the harbour, used more or less exclusively by the fishermen and the crews from the lighthouse tender and the mail boats. It was an authentic howff.

They went out in his car to the golf club, which had its own exclusiveness. It was used as a drinking place in the evenings by the professional and business people in the town. He was introduced to a number of them by Christine and found them sociable and interested. By late evening he was inclined to take a mellow view of his first day in Glendoran. A summer here might be tolerable.

They stopped at the hotel where Duthie was staying for a day or two, until he could find rooms, for coffee and a last drink. Then they walked to Christine's flat, in a large converted villa on one of the hills overlooking the town. It was getting on towards two in the morning. As he walked back to the hotel

Duthie saw a police car turning in to the fish quay. The quay was brightly lit. Some of the boats that had been out during the day were landing their catches.

The police car drove slowly along the quay, nosing between the big lorries, and stopped. Sergeant McKechnie and a young constable got out. McKechnie was a big, affable man in his forties. He stood by the car, watching the lights of a boat approaching across the bay. She had her worklights on, flooding the deck with brilliance. As she drew nearer, work on the quay stopped. The winches and the derricks were silent, leaving only the undertone of diesels throbbing below decks and the remote sounds of the town. Men talked quietly. McKechnie could see the name on her bows now – *The Maid of Lorne*. A few yards out her engine was throttled back and she drifted in to the quay and docked gently. Men on the quay took the mooring lines and made them fast.

McKechnie walked to the edge of the quay as James Campbell came up an iron ladder from her deck. His face was grey with exhaustion.

'We got your message, James,' McKechnie said gently.

James said, 'I've lost my son.'

'I know. I'm very sorry about it. What happened?'

'I don't know, Malcolm. He just went over the side. Nobody saw him go.'

McKechnie took his arm and led him across the quay towards the police car.

Christine was sitting at her desk. Duthie was sitting on a corner of the desk, reading a page of typescript. McKechnie stood back a little, watching Duthie. They had met for the first time five minutes ago. Duthie laid the typescript on the desk.

'These are the breach of the peace jobs?'

Christine said, 'Yes.'

'When's the next court?'

'Tomorrow morning.'

'Make out the complaints and I'll sign them.'

Christine nodded. Duthie looked at McKechnie.

'D'you want them in custody, Sergeant?'

'No need, Mr Duthie,' McKechnie said. 'We know where they are. They're regular customers.'

'Good,' said Duthie. 'Anything else?'

McKechnie said, 'You'll have heard there was an accident in one of the boats?'

Christine looked up at McKechnie and Duthie said, 'No.'

'*The Maid of Lorne*. They lost the mate overboard. He was the skipper's son.'

'When was this?' Duthie asked.

'About eight o'clock last night. They were trawling off one of the islands, about four hours out from here.'

'In our district?'

'Oh, yes. We'll get statements during the day and we'll put a report in to you. I had a word with the skipper last night when he came in.'

'Did he tell you what happened?'

'He doesn't know what happened. Nobody saw it.'

'Body?'

'Not recovered,' said McKechnie.

Duthie brooded for a moment, then he looked at McKechnie curiously.

'Why did you call it an accident?'

McKechnie hesitated. 'Well . . . what else?'

Duthie said, 'I don't know. But if nobody saw it, and there's no body . . .'

McKechnie gave him a comforting smile. 'It happens, Mr Duthie. It's a dangerous business, the fishing. It just happens.'

Christine said, 'I suppose it'll be a Fatal Accident Inquiry.'

McKechnie frowned and said, 'Would it not be the Board of Trade, or whatever they call themselves now? There was that other time – you remember, the lighthouse keeper . . .'

'If he was an employed person,' Duthie said, 'there must be an FAI. It says so in the book. Where's the boat now?'

'Lying at the fish quay,' said McKechnie.

'Who owns her?'

'She's what they call a family boat. Owned by the family. And most of the crew are family.'

'Skipper?'

'James Campbell. He's on the Town Council.' He grinned and added, 'But he's a very respectable man. I know James well.'

Duthie said, 'I'd like to take a look at the boat.'

McKechnie frowned again and said, 'Wouldn't it be a good idea to wait till we put in a report?'

'No, it wouldn't,' Duthie said. 'I haven't done any fishing since I went out in short pants to catch minnows with a net. I'd like to know more about it.'

McKechnie said, 'Well, I'll lay on a car for you.'

'It's not far,' Duthie said. 'I'll walk.'

'It would be as well to have one of us with you. Just to let them know who you are.'

'Otherwise they won't talk? Fair enough. We'll meet on the quay? Two o'clock?'

'That will be fine, Mr Duthie.'

When McKechnie had gone Christine looked at Duthie and asked, 'You think it wasn't an accident?'

'Come off it, love,' Duthie said. 'I never said that. I don't know what it was.'

Duthie dropped into the small pub in the back street near the harbour on his way down to the quay. He had no particular reason for doing so, except that it was on the way and some instinct nudged his elbow as he was passing it. There were only two men in it, talking quietly together at the far end of the bar. At first Duthie could hear nothing of what they were saying. The barman gave Duthie his drink, talked to him for a few moments about nothing, with Highland courtesy, then rejoined the other two.

'I hear there was a fight,' he said.

'It wasn't really a fight,' one of the men said. 'They just took a poke or two at each other.'

'Ian and Hughie?'

'I couldn't say for sure. We were two or three hundred yards away at the time. But who else would it be?'

The second man said, 'Ay, there's no love lost between those

37

two.' He drained his glass. 'Have you time for one more?'

The first man said, 'Not for me. I have to work on the net. We'll have to put a new panel in.'

He finished his drink, and after a moment or two they left together.

'Off the fishing boats?' Duthie asked.

The barman said, 'Yes,' and began to wash glasses.

Duthie persisted. 'The one that had the accident? What was her name? *The Maid of Lorne?*'

'No,' said the barman.

'You don't happen to know what boat they do come from?'

'It might be *The Good Intent*,' the barman said, without looking at him. 'But there's a good few boats in just now. It could be any one of them.'

The man was hedging. The name meant nothing to Duthie anyhow, but he filed it. He finished his drink and left, and found McKechnie waiting for him on the quay. They went down one of the iron ladders on the side of the quay to the deck of *The Maid of Lorne*. James Campbell came along the waist by the side of the wheelhouse to meet them. He looked older and less solid. His weathered skin had gone sallow. He was wearing a dark lounge suit and a black tie.

'This is Mr Duthie,' said McKechnie. 'From the Procurator Fiscal's office. He's wanting to ask you a few questions.'

Duthie said, 'I'm sorry to bother you at this time, Mr Campbell. But I'd like to get the facts while they're still fresh.'

'I understand,' said James. 'It has to be sorted out. Now's as good a time as any.'

'Can you tell me what happened?'

James made a vague, helpless gesture. 'I wish I could. But I just don't know, Mr Duthie. It's like a bad dream.'

'I'm sure it is,' Duthie said. 'I understand it happened about eight o'clock?'

'Yes.'

'What were you doing? I mean all of you. The crew as a whole.'

'We were fishing for herring. Pair fishing. Two boats with the trawl between them.'

'What was the weather like?'

'Fresh at that time. It got worse later. We'd had two or three good shots. We shot again just before eight. Then the net fouled. There's a lot of old wrecks in that part, some of them not marked on the charts. You can never be sure.'

'So what did you do?'

'Well, we steamed back over the net a couple of times to try and clear it. But it was held fast. I didn't want to lose it. They cost a lot of money, you know. Hundreds of pounds. And with the movement of the boat it would be getting damaged. So I decided to cut my warps and see if the other boat could get it away.'

'Warps?' said Duthie.

'Do you know anything about fishing?' James asked.

'Nothing.'

James took him forward and showed him the big drums on the winch with the remains of the steel warps on them, the ends roughly severed. He showed how fairleads and rollers led the warps aft along the side of the boat, over the block on the gallows near the stern and out over the side.

'Two warps, of course. One for the top of the net, one for the bottom. We had to cut both. So I sent Ian to get the wire-cutters.' He was silent for a moment. Then he said, 'I never saw him again.'

Duthie asked, after a decent pause, 'Where were the wire-cutters kept?'

James showed him the ready-use locker on the deck in front of the wheelhouse. It was standing open and Duthie could see that it now contained nothing resembling the sort of wire-cutters that would be necessary for a job like this.

'Where are they now?' he asked.

'He must have taken them over the side with him,' James said, in a low voice.

Duthie looked around. He found it surprising that a man could fall over the side in a boat like this, with comparatively little superstructure, without anybody seeing it happen.

'Why did nobody see him?' he asked. 'Where was every-body?'

James said, 'Two of the hands were down in the fish hold. James McColl had the wheel. My son Willie and me were trying to get a bit of slack on the warps at the gallows so that they wouldn't spring back on us when we cut them. McPhail, the engineer, would be coming aft from the winch about that time to help us.'

Duthie said quickly, 'Wouldn't he see anything? He'd be able to see down both sides of the wheelhouse, wouldn't he?'

'He'd be too busy stepping over the boards of the fish pounds and trying to keep his feet. He'd a problem with that at the best of times.'

'Not a good seaman?'

'Not even a good engineer.'

'What about James McColl? Wouldn't he see anything from the wheelhouse?'

'He would be looking out of the window at this side. He would be watching us. And *The Good Intent* – to keep the strain off the net.'

'*The Good Intent?*'

'The other boat.'

Duthie was silent for a moment. Coincidence? he wondered. Instinct, he decided. I'll make a good cop yet, if I ever get round to it.

'So Ian must have gone over the other side?' he said at length.

'The port side, yes.'

'Why didn't he shout?'

'Maybe he did. There was a fair bit of wind and we were on the weather side. We didn't hear him, anyhow.'

'What happened when he didn't come back?'

'I sent Willie to find out why he was taking so long. Then we cut the warps with a cold chisel and began to look for him.'

Duthie said, 'Is Willie on board? Could I speak to him?'

James hesitated. 'Go easy with him, Mr Duthie,' he said after a moment. 'He's taking it hard.'

'Of course,' Duthie said.

James went to the head of the ladder that led down to the mess deck and called, and after a moment or two the boy came up. He was nervous and wary, but he told his story clearly and without fumbling, almost as though he had rehearsed it. And why not? Duthie thought. He must have had a rough night, remembering it.

There had been no trace of Ian, on the forward deck or on the port side of the wheelhouse. He had called down into the fish hold. He had gone down into the mess decks and engine space, then he had reported back to his father.

'Was the sea rough?' Duthie asked.

Willie shrugged. 'Kind of.'

'Could your brother swim?'

James said, 'He was wearing oilskins and seaboots,' and left it at that.

'Was he a good seaman?'

'He was a fine seaman. It was his life for seventeen years. Before that he was often out with me as a young boy.'

'In all kinds of weather?'

'The worst, sometimes.'

'Worse than yesterday evening?'

'I told you. Yesterday was just a bit fresh.'

Duthie said, 'But he never fell over the side before.'

James gave him a hard look and Duthie felt a faint twinge of contrition, which was unusual.

'I'm told this is a family boat,' he said. 'Owned by the family?'

'Some of the family have shares in her,' James said carefully, and for the first time Duthie felt he was being a little devious.

'Crewed by the family?' he asked.

'Me, Ian and Willie. McPhail's my nephew – my wife's nephew. And there's three spare hands not related.'

'Thank you,' said Duthie. 'You've been very patient.'

As they moved towards the ladder, McPhail came down it from the quay.

'This is my nephew, Hugh McPhail,' said James. 'This is Mr Duthie, Hughie.'

Duthie was looking at the dark, contused area above McPhail's right eye.

'That's a nasty bruise, Mr McPhail.'

'I had a fall when we were coming in last night. I'm not too good on my feet when there's a sea running.'

'So I've been told,' said Duthie.

McPhail gave him a brief nod and went aft.

James watched Duthie until he had left the quay in the police car, then he went down to the mess. It was small, warm and thick with the smell of coffee.

'I'll take a cup, Willie,' he said, and sat down opposite McPhail. He studied the bruise on McPhail's forehead. 'Willie will give you a bit of steak out of the fridge. It'll take down the swelling.'

McPhail nodded.

James said, 'Where do you suppose the wire-cutters are, Hughie?'

'Don't ask me. We looked for them last night and didn't find them.'

'Over the side, do you think? With Ian.'

McPhail shrugged and said nothing.

'If he found them in the locker,' James said, 'why didn't he come straight back with them to the gallows, where we were waiting? Why would he go over to the far side of the boat?'

'Maybe they weren't in the locker.'

James frowned. 'Ian was particular about that kind of thing. Everything in its place. They were in it earlier when I was looking for a new shackle-pin for the sweep.'

'One of the boys could have moved them.'

'I'll have to ask them,' said James. Willie gave him a thick mug of coffee, and he sat with it in his hands for a time, brooding. 'After all these years, out in all kinds of weather, and we lose Ian on a day when there was no real reason for it. It's a strange thing.' He looked up at McPhail. 'Wouldn't you think so, Hughie?'

'Ay.'

'What I'm afraid of is that he's no fool, that chap.'

McPhail looked at him sharply.

'Who?'

'Mr Duthie,' said James.

IV

McKechnie came into the office with Duthie when they got back. They were polite to each other, but Christine sensed that they had been arguing. She knew McKechnie well as an equable and kindly man, but at the moment there was a tightness about his mouth that she had seen only once or twice before. Certain types of crime induced it, like the mistreatment of children. She looked at Duthie curiously. What *have* you been doing? she thought.

'I suppose you want tea,' she said. Duthie nodded, and she went into the cupboard and put on the kettle.

Duthie waved McKechnie to a chair. McKechnie put his cap on top of a filing cabinet but remained on his feet.

Duthie said, 'There was something between them.'

'McPhail and the deceased?'

'Yes.'

'Like what?'

'I don't know. But they had a fight, anyhow.'

'You said yourself, Mr Duthie – the man said it wasn't really a fight, they just took a poke at each other.'

'It comes to the same thing.'

'Not at all!' McKechnie said, with a touch of impatience. 'It's a tough life. Tempers get frayed. Maybe they do get into a fight from time to time. Maybe about nothing that matters. So afterwards they shake hands.'

'A damn rough kind of handshake. Ian Campbell won't recover from it.'

McKechnie started to say something but thought better of it as Christine came out of the cupboard with three mugs and the Georgian silver on a tin tray. She laid the tray on a corner of her desk, left them to help themselves and sat down.

'Besides,' said Duthie, 'he was covering up. Why didn't he tell me about the fight or whatever you want to call it? He must have known about it. It happened on the open deck. It was seen from the other boat.'

43

McKechnie said, 'He may not have considered it to be relevant.'

'Oh, for God's sake!' Duthie said with sudden impatience. 'He'd lost his son in mysterious circumstances. A good seaman goes over the side in moderate weather, doing nothing dramatic, just fetching a cutting tool from a locker on the deck. Don't you think he wants to know why? Don't you think he's been churning over in his mind every damned thing that happened last night?'

McKechnie thought about it for a moment. 'Yes, I suppose you're right, Mr Duthie. But I wouldn't have thought James Campbell would lie to you. I've known him for a long time.'

'I'm not suggesting he did. But I think he knows more than he told me.'

Christine looked up from her desk and said, 'Anyhow, Mr Sutherland will be back tomorrow.'

Duthie stared at her for a moment, then he grinned. Christine was annoyed to find herself colouring.

Duthie said, 'Admirably clear, Miss Russell. But a little tactless.'

McKechnie laughed. 'We'll have the report on your desk tomorrow, Mr Duthie. We'll cover the points you've mentioned.'

'I'm sure you will. Please don't think I'm trying to interfere.'

'Not at all,' said McKechnie. 'It's your job, after all.'

He picked up his hat from the filing cabinet and moved towards the door.

'I don't suppose you happen to know,' Duthie said, 'where the widow lives?'

Janet Campbell lived in a substantial modern bungalow in a well-to-do development of similar houses on the edge of the town. The front lawn was manicured, the footpaths paved, a short tarmacadam drive led to a garage with an up-and-over door, now open, revealing the back end of a Rover 2000. It may be a tough life, Duthie thought, but there's loot in it. He turned off the drive, along a paved path, to the front door. A window was open. Chintz curtains billowed gently in the mild spring air, and inside a radio was playing. Light music. Duthie pressed the bell. Chimes sounded, the music stopped suddenly and after a moment the door opened.

Janet Campbell was around thirty, pretty, blonde and a little brassy, pale faced and dark round the eyes. She was composed but under considerable emotional stress; but Duthie had the odd impression that cheerfulness might break through at the slightest provocation.

He introduced himself. She glanced past him at the police car waiting out on the road and invited him to come in. She took him into a sitting-room furnished with stuff that was modern, angular and probably expensive. She was nervous.

'It's too bad we have to trouble you at a time like this,' Duthie said, as he offered her a cigarette and lit it for her.

'That's all right.'

'It must have been a dreadful shock.'

'Yes, it was.'

Duthie had a talent for exuding warmth and sympathy when the occasion required it. He had practised it many years ago with maiden aunts in Hawick. Janet Campbell was nobody's maiden aunt, but the principle was the same.

'But in a way, you know,' she said, 'it wasn't.'

'You mean it wasn't entirely unexpected?'

'It's just the life. Every time they go out you have to face the fact that something like this can happen. If I'd known what it was like I don't think I'd ever have married into it. Sometimes I never saw Ian for more than two or three hours at a time for weeks on end.'

'You don't belong here, do you?'

'No, I'm Glasgow. D'you know Glasgow?'

'Well enough,' said Duthie, an Edinburgh man. 'I'm told it's different here.'

'It certainly is.'

'Boring?'

Janet said, 'It's not bad in the summer. But in the winter . . .'

'The incest belt?'

She gave him a pale smile. 'How long have you been here?'

'A day or two.'

'You're very perceptive.'

Duthie said, 'I have an imagination that sometimes runs riot. It's not supposed to be a good thing in my job.'

She laughed and relaxed a little more. Duthie let her talk. It seemed to be doing her good and it was producing some useful information. She was a nice enough woman, but lost; she had married into a community and a background for which she had neither sympathy nor understanding. She was now full of small resentments, not least against her late husband. It was hard to understand how she had ever married him. Duthie surmised that she had come up to Glendoran once for a holiday and fallen for his yellow oilskins.

'I'll be all right, of course,' she said. 'There's the house and the car, and there's money in the bank. But you'd have thought Ian would have a share in the boat, wouldn't you? The eldest son.'

'Didn't he?'

'No, he didn't. And I could never get him to do anything about it. My father-in-law's not the easiest of men, whatever you may have heard about him.'

'I've heard he's highly respected.'

'Oh, yes. A pillar of the kirk and all that. You know how they work the money in the boats?'

'No.'

'Half what they get from the catch goes to the boat. Paying it off, cost of running, keeping up the nets, that sort of thing. They divide the other half equally between the crew. The skipper gets the same as the others.'

'That seems fair enough.'

'Except that the boat's worth eighty thousand pounds. And it belongs to the skipper.'

'Nobody else?'

'Not that I know of.'

Duthie brooded for a moment. Some of the family have shares in her, Campbell had said. The skipper's wife, perhaps. But not the son who sailed and worked in her.

'Your father-in-law may have thought they were all getting good money out of her. And presumably she'd have passed to

46

your husband eventually. Did Ian ever complain?'

'No,' she said. 'Except . . .' She thought for a moment. 'Well, he did, a bit, during the past two or three months. He seemed kind of angry all the time. Frustrated, if you know what I mean.'

She could not enlarge on this. But it seemed that for some time her husband had been moody and querulous and that she thought it had something to do with the boat. Presently Duthie rose to leave.

'I'm sorry I had to bother you.'

'If there's anything else . . .'

'I'll come back,' said Duthie. 'What happened to Hughie?'

She gave him a look of utter astonishment.

'That's a nasty bruise on his forehead,' Duthie said.

'Oh, that,' she said. She took a slow breath. 'Yes, it is, isn't it? He had a fall on the way home last night. It's just that he's not as used to it as the others.'

Duthie watched the colour coming back into her cheeks. Poor lassie, he thought. She has no guile in her. She's just bored and a little stupid. He gave her a friendly smile, said goodbye, and walked along the paved path and down the tarmacadam drive to the waiting police car.

Sutherland arrived back the following morning as unobtrusively as a Caribbean hurricane hitting the Florida coast. He had been sniffing the West Highland air for the past thirty miles or so, and was now restored after two nights in Edinburgh, a city for which he had no affection. He said good morning to Christine, passed briskly through the main office and threw his briefcase on to a chair in his own room. He was already sitting behind the desk when Christine came in with a handful of letters and papers.

'Good morning,' she said. 'Had a good trip?'

'Predictable. Boring speeches and a bed that was too short for me. Everything all right here?'

'Yes, I think so. More or less.'

Sutherland looked up from the papers she had given him.

'Mr Duthie thinks he's found a murder,' she said.

Sutherland sat back and stared at her. 'Isn't that a little

greedy? Surely a couple of rapes would have been sufficient for a man who's only been here for forty-eight hours?'

She smiled and touched a manilla folder on his desk.

'It's all in here. He thought you might like to look through his notes.'

'That's remarkably kind of him,' Sutherland said. He picked up the folder and leafed through it. 'He's in court, I suppose?'

'Yes.'

'Would it be an intrusion if we asked him to spare me a few moments when he's dealt with the Sheriff?'

Christine laughed and said, 'I don't think so. He's very approachable.'

Duthie had had a routine but moderately pleasant morning. Sheriff Derwent had been in an affable mood and they had had one or two agreeably brittle exchanges. When the court rose Duthie stayed to chat for a few moments with Liz Hamilton, remarking that he was not normally in the habit of doing so with Sheriff Clerks, who were usually greyish men with no time to spare. Then he went downstairs, whistling. He met Cairns, the usher, coming up.

'You did fine, Mr Duthie. The Sheriff likes a bit of backchat now and again.'

'Thanks,' said Duthie.

Cairns said, 'As long as you don't overdo it,' and continued upstairs.

Christine looked up from her work as Duthie came in.

'Mr Sutherland's back.'

'Oh, good,' said Duthie.

'I'm glad you feel that way about it,' she said pleasantly. 'He'd be obliged if you could spare him a moment or two.'

Duthie laid his papers on Christine's desk, dropped his gown over the back of a chair, knocked on Sutherland's door and went in.

Sutherland laid aside the manilla folder and said, 'Good morning, Mr Duthie.'

He was wearing spectacles and looked distinguished.

Duthie said, 'Good morning, sir.'

48

'You've kicked off with a monstrous blast on the trumpet,' Sutherland said.

Duthie grinned a little uneasily.

Sutherland said, 'I've just had the Chief Inspector on the phone. He tells me you've been prodding poor McKechnie.'

'To be honest, I have a bit. I felt I ought to. Nothing against McKechnie. He's been very helpful. But I just wanted to get at the background before it got—' he floundered for words and went on, 'Before it got soft round the edges.'

Sutherland took off his glasses, looked at him in silence for a moment, then pointed with the glasses at a comfortable arm-chair.

'Sit down. Unburden yourself. I've read your notes. I know that Ian Campbell was lost over the side and that nobody saw him go. Now what's it all about?'

Duthie sat down and said, 'I think he was pushed.'

'I take it you think you know who pushed him.'

'There was some kind of fight earlier in the evening between Ian Campbell and McPhail.'

'What about?'

'I don't know yet. But there was bad blood between them. I don't know the reason for it, but I've got ideas.'

'Can you prove them?'

'Not at the moment.'

'Could you prove there was a fight?'

'I doubt it. I think everybody who saw it will say there wasn't one.'

'You're too subtle for me.'

'I think they're covering up for McPhail.'

'Who is?'

'James Campbell, for one.'

'Why should he?'

'I don't know. I assume McPhail's got some kind of hold.'

'Why do you assume that?'

'It's just a hunch at the moment.'

'Are you subject to hunches?'

'Yes.'

'God help us. Are you suggesting blackmail?'

49

Duthie thought for a moment. 'I wouldn't put it as high as that. More a question of not treading on his toes.'

'And as for the others?'

Duthie shrugged. 'I don't think they'll want to give anything away to outsiders. The clan closing ranks, sort of thing.'

'It's an ingenious concoction. But it won't work. What was your impression of James Campbell?'

'Straight.'

'Quite right. If Campbell says Ian was alone when he went over the side, that is what he believes. What's more, a local jury and the Sheriff will believe it too.'

'You mean we can't win?'

Sutherland said: 'We never win. You should know that. We have no triumphs. A case proves or it doesn't. The truth is discovered. Or remains hidden. We sometimes fail. But our failures are when justice is not served.'

After a moment Duthie said, 'I'm sorry. I deserved that. I expect you want to take this out of my hands.'

Sutherland looked at him for several seconds without speaking. Then he said, 'This is your baby, Alexander. I'm not an obstetrician. You can damn well deliver it yourself.'

McKechnie was waiting in the main office when Duthie came out of Sutherland's room. He had some information which he thought might be of interest.

Duthie said, 'Come on in,' and led the way into his room. McKechnie followed and closed the door carefully.

Duthie said, 'I'm sorry I pushed you. My trouble is that I'm still young and brash.'

McKechnie laughed and said, 'I'll bear that in mind, Mr Duthie.'

'Pull up one of these delightful plastic-covered metal chairs,' said Duthie, 'and make yourself comfortable.'

'No offence, Mr Duthie. I'll stand . . . You were asking about who had a share in the boat.'

'Yes.'

'It's Hugh McPhail. He has a quarter share.'

Duthie said nothing.

'You're not surprised?' said McKechnie.

'You couldn't knock me down with a feather. How did he get it?'

'It seems she had to have a new engine a few months ago. They're always needing to increase the power in these boats. James Campbell isn't the man to dip a hand into his pocket if he can help it. So Hughie agreed to put up the money.'

'Where did he find it?'

'He had a wee garage left him by his father. It wasn't doing too well. So he sold out and put the money into *The Maid of Lorne*.'

'And signed on as engineer?'

'That's right.'

'About three months ago?'

McKechnie looked at him sharply. 'You're well informed.'

'I get hunches,' Duthie said.

But he felt it a reasonable supposition that Ian Campbell's period of frustration and querulousness began when Hugh McPhail started to acquire an interest in the boat. And remembering Janet Campbell's curious reaction he wondered if McPhail, before that, had not perhaps been taking over a share in more than the boat, while Ian was at sea for long hours, while his wife was bored and discontented, and while McPhail was letting his garage business slide downhill. Duthie knew that he was reaching, and said so.

McKechnie said, 'It's jumping to conclusions, Mr Duthie. I've known Mr Sutherland for a long time, and he doesn't like this sort of thing at all.'

'I've only known him for forty-eight hours,' said Duthie, 'but I'm quite sure you're right.'

'All the same,' said McKechnie, 'do you know what I saw in Glendoran this morning?' He paused for effect, watching Duthie with a quizzical light in his eyes.

'No,' said Duthie. 'Tell me.'

'I saw McPhail driving through the town in a Rover 2000. Now isn't that a queer thing?'

'Does he own one?'

'No, no. It was Ian Campbell's. Mrs Campbell's now, I suppose. I had the registration checked.'

Duthie got to his feet and began to prowl round the room.

'Then it hangs together. McPhail was taking over. Probably the wife. Certainly the boat. Ian may not have known about the wife, though he may have suspected. But he would surely know that his cousin – that's right, isn't it?'

McKechnie nodded, and Duthie went on.

'That his cousin had taken over a part of his patrimony. That's enough to create bad blood. It makes the alleged fight or whatever it was reasonably credible. Did you get anything more about that?'

'No. All that any of them would say was that McPhail wasn't handling the winch right and Ian pushed him away from it.'

'What about the men in the other boat?'

'It was dark, Mr Duthie, and they were too far away. We'd never get them to swear to a positive identification.'

'I don't suppose so,' Duthie said. 'I think we've got enough all the same to justify making some assumptions.'

'Maybe we have,' McKechnie said slowly. 'But . . .'

'Yes, I know,' said Duthie. 'It's the wrong way round. It's McPhail that should have gone over the side.'

He prowled for a moment or two, brooding, and then said suddenly: 'You know what I think happened? I think Ian was nursing jealousy and anger for some time. I think it came to a head when there was some kind of a fight early in the evening, which was cooled off by the others. But I think it broke out again later, when everybody was busy trying to save the net. It could have happened on the port side of the wheelhouse. Nobody would see it from the gallows on the starboard side, or from the fish hold. Nobody would hear it with a big diesel thumping away under their feet and the wind blowing in the wrong direction. And Ian and McPhail were the only two men whose position was not precisely known. Ian had gone to get the wire-cutters. McPhail was – Skipper Campbell said – on his way aft.'

McKechnie thought for a moment, then said, 'I've got a

feeling you're making your facts fit your theory, Mr Duthie.'

Duthie said, 'They do fit, though.'

'They fit all right. But I doubt if you'll ever prove them.'

'Not directly. But if McPhail got his face from a left hook and not from a fall, somebody's covering for him. The skipper. Why? I didn't get the impression that anybody likes McPhail particularly. What kind of a hold hàs he got, apart from owning a bit of the boat?'

'There's no one in Glendoran will have the kind of hold you're talking about on James Campbell. He's a solid man.'

'How long has he been in Glendoran?'

'About fifteen years. The family came here from Drumbaan. A fishing village on the Firth of Clyde.'

'Yes, I've heard of it. Why did they leave there?'

'I would have said because the herring were leaving that area. But they'd been leaving it for a dozen years before that.'

'Could you make enquiries? Nothing specific. Just general background?'

McKechnie hesitated. 'Well, we could, certainly. But it's a long time ago. And I don't see where it could connect with Hughie. He's been a Glendoran man all his life.'

Duthie said, 'I know. It's a long shot. But I think it's worth trying.'

When McKechnie had gone, Duthie returned to his desk and sat down. He went over the thing again in his mind. There were some pieces left over, but the jigsaw seemed to fit together well enough and he was reasonably satisfied. He was unaware of a cloud the size of a man's hand that had begun to appear beyond the distant horizon.

Angus McInnes sat with it in his hands on a bench that he had built in front of the house. It was a long envelope, with his name and address neatly typed on it, very formal looking. The address pleased him: Camas Dearg. That was the name of the little bay down below where he was going to keep his boat. It came from the red sandstone rocks. It had not occurred to him as a suitable name for the house, which he had not yet named at all. He opened the envelope, pulled out the contents slightly and saw that they consisted of a printed form, with a great deal of small print. It was a day of pearl grey sunlight, promising warmth later, with the cormorants flying low over the water and the big heron standing like a statue out on the point. Earlier, a young seal had been playing around the island. It was no day for small print; so he pushed the thing back into the envelope, took it inside and placed it with other correspondence under the tea caddy on the mantelpiece. He picked up a stick with a handle of finely carved horn and went out again. He called the dog, and they walked down the hill together to the shores of the bay, Camas Dearg, where he would spend an hour or two deciding where he would lay down the mooring for the boat.

By the date set for the Fatal Accident Inquiry into the death of Ian Campbell no enlightening information had arrived from Drumbaan. Duthie suspected that no great pressure had been put on the local police, but McKechnie assured him that enquiries had been made in line with his instructions. They were still in hand. Something might yet turn up, though it might be too late to have any bearing.

Duthie mentioned it to Sutherland, who seemed a little off hand about it.

'We've called all the witnesses,' he said. 'One of them – McPhail, for example – may hold the key. If you can break him down we'll know what happened.'

'If,' said Duthie.

'Exactly. It's a matter of luck. Archie Derwent carries two principal banners. One for Truth. The other for The Rights of Witnesses. Unfortunately, we never know in advance which one he's flying on any particular day.'

Duthie was to discover that today was close season for witnesses.

The public benches were well filled as the Sheriff Clerk's pleasant contralto called the names of the jury.

'Ladies and gentlemen, please stand when your names are called and remain standing until you have taken the oath . . . Alan McPhee . . . James Rankin . . . John Gray . . .'

Duthie watched the pale morning sunlight bringing out the highlights in the Sheriff Clerk's dark, glossy hair, and thought, 'What a waste, a girl like that in a place like this. And yet, what a consolation on a day such as this is probably going to be.' The Sheriff sat with his eyes on his notebook, in which he was drawing a fishing boat in a rough sea. Cairns, the usher, stood by the swing doors with a vacant look on his face, trying to tot up the number of FAIs he had attended in this court since his retirement twenty years ago from the Metropolitan Police. He had got to twenty-three when the Sheriff Clerk called the last of the jurors.

'Ian Gillespie . . . Ronald Stevenson . . . Catherine Dunlop,' she said, and glanced round at Duthie as though she had read his thoughts. Duthie moved uneasily, and she turned back to the seven jurors, now standing.

'Will you each hold up your right hand,' she said, and they did so. 'You seven swear by Almighty God and as you shall answer to God at the Great Day of Judgement, that you will truth say and no truth conceal in so far as you are to pass on the inquiry assigned for today.'

The jurors mumbled agreements and Liz Hamilton said, 'Please be seated.'

She picked up a sheet of paper from the table in front of her and read: 'The inquiry today relates to the death of Ian Peter Campbell, of 23 Crombie Place, in this town, who did, in the course of his employment as mate in the fishing vessel *Maid of Lorne*, fall into the sea at about eight o'clock on the evening of fifteenth May and is presumed drowned.'

She sat down. There was a brief silence. A solicitor sitting opposite Duthie rose to his feet, a plump, merry, shrewd, elderly man, much at home in this court.

'My lord, I represent Mr James Campbell and –' he glanced at Duthie over his spectacles '– and Mr Hugh McPhail.'

He sat down again. The Sheriff said, 'Thank you, Mr Robertson,' and looked at Duthie.

Duthie rose and said, 'My lord, *The Maid of Lorne* is a diesel fishing vessel of eighty feet in length and eighteen feet six inches beam. She is engaged in trawling in middle – as distinct

55

from distant or inshore – waters. On fifteenth May she was fishing for herring off the eastern shore of the island of Ornsay. It was here that the deceased met his death. With your lordship's permission I would like to refer to two incidents which occurred earlier in the day. One a short time before the boat sailed from the fish quay at Glendoran on that day. The other in the early evening when they were shooting the net for the first time.'

'What kind of incidents?' asked the Sheriff.

'They were disagreements, my lord,' said Duthie carefully.

'Involving the deceased?'

'Yes, my lord.'

'Very well. Go on.'

Duthie went on.

Christine came out of the filing cupboard with the tea tray as Sutherland came out of his office with a number of manilla folders which he laid on Christine's desk.

'None of these is urgent,' he said.

Christine said, 'That makes a change.'

She cleared a space and put the tray down.

'Except the report to the Crown Office,' Sutherland added. 'That should go off today.'

He picked up a mug of tea from the tray and sugared it.

'What are you worried about?'

She looked at him quickly. 'Me? Nothing.'

'Duthie is perfectly capable of conducting a Fatal Accident Inquiry.'

'I didn't say he wasn't.'

'It's early to judge whether he's a little too impetuous for the Fiscal Service. It calls for a particular attitude. He'll make a lot of mistakes. Beat his head painfully against a number of brick walls. Irritate many people, especially myself. But he may settle down. And he doesn't need anybody to hold his hand in the meantime.'

'I don't suppose he does.'

'However, if you feel the urge and have the time to spare, by all means go up and do so.'

She decided not to be drawn. So she smiled and said, 'It might embarrass him. And he's got enough on his hands as it is.'

'You sailed from the fish quay at about two o'clock that afternoon,' Duthie said. 'Am I correct?'

James Campbell was in the witness box, facing him. His strong brown hands rested lightly on the brass rail.

'Quite correct, Mr Duthie.'

'Hugh McPhail is your engineer?'

'Yes.'

'Am I right in thinking he came down to the boat at about noon that morning?'

'At about noon, yes.'

'Was there an incident on the quay as he came on board?'

James frowned and scratched the back of his head.

'What kind of an incident, Mr Duthie?'

'Did he fall?'

James's face cleared.

'You're right enough. So he did.'

'How did he fall?'

'He tripped over a mooring line.'

'What caused him to trip over a mooring line?'

James smiled.

'It's just one of Hughie's problems, Mr Duthie. I never saw a man with as many left feet.'

'Apart from anatomical deviations,' Duthie said, and won himself a wintry smile from the Sheriff, 'was he pushed?'

'Well, I couldn't really say, Mr Duthie. I was in the boat at the time, and the deck was eight or ten feet below the quay.'

'If you couldn't see whether he was pushed or not, how can you know that he tripped?'

'If you knew Hughie as well as I do,' James said, 'you would agree that it's a reasonable supposition.'

Duthie said, a little sharply, 'I think you saw him being pushed. Did you not say: "That was a daft thing to do. You might have broken his neck"?'

James gave Duthie a surprised look and hesitated.

The Sheriff glanced at Robertson. Robertson's eyes twinkled merrily behind his spectacles, and the Sheriff looked at Duthie.

'Come, come, Mr Duthie. You are trying to get the witness to say that he had said what you would have liked him to have said, are you not?'

Duthie considered this for a moment and decided that it would be dangerous to get involved. He said, 'Thank you, my lord. I appreciate your argument,' and began again.

He turned back to James. 'Would it be correct to say that you reached the fishing ground and shot your trawl for the first time that day at about seven o'clock?'

'That would be correct.'

'Did an incident concerning the operation of the winch occur at this time?'

Again James looked surprised. He thought for a moment. He had been right, then. Duthie was no fool.

'Hugh McPhail was at the winch,' he said. 'He was supposed to be keeping a tension on the warps. But he was letting them out too fast and my son Ian went forward to check him.'

'Did they get into an argument about it?'

'My son remonstrated.'

'Was there a fight?'

'You can't do much fighting when you're all wrapped up in oilskins.'

Robertson said mildly, 'A technical discussion, surely.'

Duthie glanced at him and said, 'Thank you.' He turned back to James. 'During this technical discussion,' he asked, 'did McPhail receive a blow which caused a large bruise above his right eye?'

'No, he did not.'

'I remind you that you're on oath.'

'I know that, Mr Duthie.'

They looked at each other for a moment, and Duthie thought: He's not lying. And that suits me.

'Where were you during the course of this technical discussion?'

'In the wheelhouse. But I got the impression that things might be getting just a wee bit heated, so I went forward.'

'And there was no sign of damage to McPhail's face at that time?'

'None.'

'But he did have a large bruise above his right eye the following day?'

'He said he got it from a fall during the passage home.'

'Did anybody see him fall?'

'Not to my knowledge. But it seems likely enough, Mr Duthie. You'll mind what I told you . . .'

'Yes, I know. But the fact is that nobody appears to have seen it. Could the . . . the technical discussion have broken out again some time later?'

'It didn't. We were too busy. We were into a good lot of fish. I would have known if any man was away from his job.'

'You told the Court earlier that the net fouled and you decided to cut the warps. There must have been some confusion at that point.'

'A bit. Not much.'

'Where was your son?'

'At the gallows with me and the boy Willie, getting in a bit of slack on the warps so that they wouldn't spring back when we cut them.'

'And McPhail?'

'At the winch. When I sent Ian to get the cutters I called Hughie aft to help me and Willie hold the slack we'd got in.'

'Did he come directly? Immediately you called him?'

'I think so.'

'You're not sure?'

'How could I be sure? How can I tell you if he came at once? I was hauling on the steel warps at the time. I wasn't looking at Hughie or anyone else. I didn't want to get my two hands crushed.'

'Is it not possible that McPhail might have . . .'

The Sheriff said suddenly, 'You're asking him to speculate, Mr Duthie. I think the witness has told you all he knows.'

Duthie said, 'My lord, I've been trying to show that . . .'

'I know what you've been trying to show, Mr Duthie. I've been listening to you carefully. But I don't think conjecture is a promising foundation on which to work. Don't you agree with me?'

'Yes, my lord.'

'Good.'

The Sheriff sat back and looked up at the light fitting shaped like a goldfish bowl and allowed himself a moment of private speculation as Duthie reorganized. What, he wondered, did Sutherland find so fascinating about it?

Duthie looked at Robertson, who smiled and shook his head. Duthie turned back to James.

'Thank you, Mr Campbell.'

The usher opened the door of the witness box and James descended from it.

Christine put her head round the door and said, 'Will you see Sergeant McKechnie?'

Sutherland nodded and McKechnie came in. He had a piece of paper in his hand.

'This just came in,' he said. 'As Mr Duthie's in court, I thought you would like to see it.'

Sutherland read the brief typewritten message, laid it on his desk and looked up.

McKechnie said, 'There was a routine report ten days ago. You'll have seen it.' Sutherland nodded and McKechnie went on, 'This seems to be a kind of afterthought that somebody has dug up.'

'It's unfortunate. But it lends some substance to Mr Duthie's theory.'

'It's certainly not the kind of skeleton,' McKechnie said, 'that anybody in his position would want dragged out of the woodpile.'

'McPhail would know, of course?'

'He's the kind of man who would ferret a thing like that out. And he's in the family, in a way.'

'All the same,' Sutherland said after a moment, 'it doesn't fit.'

'No. Not exactly. It wouldn't work, I don't think, with a man like James Campbell. Not as I know him.'

Sutherland looked at his watch. 'They'll adjourn for lunch any time now. We'll discuss this with Mr Duthie. And see if you can waylay Skipper Campbell. Tell him I'd be obliged if he'd stick around.'

McKechnie nodded and went out.

Sutherland picked up the piece of paper and brooded over it.

Duthie had had a bad hour. McPhail was shrewd enough to see which banner the Sheriff was carrying today, and made good use of it. By lunch time the Sheriff was irritable and petulant; much of the twinkle had gone from the bright eyes behind Robertson's spectacles; the jury were restless; but what worried Duthie most was the Sheriff Clerk. He had never before met a woman like Liz Hamilton who had looked at him with a maternal expression. He knew then that he was lost.

He came down from the courtroom and found McKechnie drinking tea in the main office. Christine told him that Sutherland was waiting for him and he went in. Sutherland handed him the message from the Drumbaan police without comment. Duthie read it and frowned.

'I thought there must be something,' he said. 'I didn't expect this.'

'Is it what you want?'

'It's not what I want in the least. But it may be what I need.'

'What do you propose to do with it?'

'Recall Campbell and introduce this.'

'You must be mad!'

Duthie looked startled. He had had a bad enough morning already.

Sutherland said, 'What does it prove? That James Campbell had a bastard seventeen years ago. That young Willie's a natural son. What about it? We're not concerned with morals.'

'McPhail would know about this, wouldn't he?'

'Probably.'

'It's something Campbell would do a lot to keep hidden. He's a pillar of society.'

'And you propose to knock him down?'

Duthie said angrily, 'Look, I know there was a second fight

61

in that boat. I believe that's when Ian went over the side. It's not the *Queen Mary*. Somebody must have seen it or heard it.'

'You think that Skipper Campbell knows about it and is yielding to pressure from McPhail?'

'On the basis that his son is dead and nothing can change that?' he added, when Duthie made no answer.

'Something like that,' Duthie admitted.

Sutherland rose and went to the door. He opened it and said to McKechnie, 'Did you get Skipper Campbell?'

'He's waiting in the Advocates' Room.'

'Ask him to come in.'

McKechnie nodded and went out. Sutherland returned to his desk. Duthie said nothing. A minute later McKechnie came in with James.

'Shut the door, Sergeant,' Sutherland said, and handed James the Drumbaan police report. 'This has been unearthed in the course of routine enquiries. No one has seen it outside this office, except the police.'

James read in silence, then laid the paper on Sutherland's desk. He took his time before he spoke.

'I'll not pretend,' he said at length, 'that I want my dirty linen washed in public. Especially when I've acquired a reputation for respectability. But it's a kind of accidental reputation, if you know what I mean. I've never pretended to be anything but what I am.'

Duthie said, 'You left Drumbaan because of this, surely?'

'My wife wanted to leave. It was difficult for her. It was of no great importance to me.'

'Does Willie know?' Sutherland asked.

'No. And I'd prefer him to find out in his own way, if he has to.'

'Does McPhail know?'

James thought for a moment. 'I couldn't tell you. It's possible, of course. And I'll not pretend there's any great affection between me and Hughie. He's a bad influence in my family.'

Duthie was about to speak, but Sutherland caught his eye and shook his head slightly.

'Who else would know? Your daughter-in-law? Mrs Ian?'

'I doubt it. She never takes any interest in anything that doesn't concern her own comfort and pleasure.'

Sutherland said, 'Mr Duthie thinks that there may have been a second . . . disagreement, at the time your son went over the side.'

James turned to Duthie and gave him a long, thoughtful look.

'And I've kept quiet about it to preserve my reputation?'

Duthie said, 'I wondered.'

'You have no son of your own, I take it?'

'No.'

'You may have some day,' James said. 'Don't misunderstand me when I say this. Whatever he's like, good, bad or indifferent, I hope for your sake you die before him.'

Duthie said nothing.

'Do you really imagine I'd have sheltered McPhail or anyone else, whatever the pressure, if I thought for a moment they'd a hand in my son's death?'

Duthie remained silent for a moment. Then he said, 'I apologize.'

James nodded and turned to the door. McKechnie opened it for him. James paused in the doorway and looked back.

'I know you're doing your best to find out what happened to Ian, Mr Duthie,' he said. 'And I thank you for it.'

He went out. McKechnie closed the door. Duthie picked up the Drumbaan report, read it again, crumpled it and tossed it into Sutherland's wastepaper basket.

'That was an official document,' Sutherland said mildly. 'However, I don't suppose it matters.'

'Did he send your brother to get the wire-cutters?' Duthie asked.

Willie Campbell carried himself well in the witness box. He was composed and his voice was steady. But the knuckles of his hands, as they gripped the brass rail, were white.

'Yes,' he said.

'And then what happened?'

'Well, my brother went. And we hung on to the warps for a while. Then the skipper called to Hughie McPhail to come and give us a hand. He had to call twice.'

'McPhail didn't hear the first time?'

'There was a good deal of noise. Gear banging about, and the sea. And we were on the weather side.'

'What next? McPhail came?'

'Well, I went to see why Ian was taking so long first.'

'Tell his lordship about that.'

'Well, I went round the forward end of the wheelhouse, where the ready-use locker was, where the wire-cutters were kept, and he wasn't there. I took a look down the fish hold, round the port side of the deckhouse, round the stern, but he wasn't there. I looked in the mess and the bunkroom, but he wasn't there. There was nowhere else he could be. So I went back to the gallows where my father was. Hughie was there now and they were hanging on to the warps, and I said "Ian's gone".'

'Was a search then started?'

'Well, yes, as soon as we could. We had to get clear of the trawl. Cut the warps. And that took a bit of time.'

The Sheriff said, 'How long did it take to cut the warps? About two minutes, perhaps?'

'Well, no, sir, it took longer than that.'

'With wire-cutters?'

'We were using a cold chisel and a hammer, sir. It takes longer.'

'I see.'

The Sheriff looked at Duthie. There was a curious light in his eyes. Almost affable, Duthie thought. And then he thought, 'The old devil!' He turned to Willie again and said casually, 'When I looked in the ready-use locker the wire-cutters weren't there.'

'Well, no, they wouldn't be, would they?' Willie said. 'That's why we had to use a cold chisel. Ian had them in his hand.'

'When he went over the side?'

Willie stared at him and was silent.

'Did you see him go over the side?' Duthie asked gently.

The colour had gone out of the western sky and the islands had lost their sharp silhouettes. The wind was fresher and the sea had got up quite a bit, and the spray was lashing at their faces as they clung to the warps. The thick gloves protecting their hands were clumsy, wet and greasy and slippery, and the warps were tugging and heaving with the movement of the boat and the sea. James McColl was doing a fine job, keeping the boat moving slightly astern so that there was no tension on the warps other than their own weight.

James called to McPhail, 'Hughie! Come back here and give us a hand! . . . Easy, Willie,' he said. 'Don't get yourself hurt. All we have to do is hang on to the slack till we get them cut . . . Hugh!' he shouted again. 'Come back aft a minute!'

'He'll never hear you in this,' Willie said.

'Go and see what's taking Ian so long,' said James. 'And tell Hughie.'

Willie hesitated and said, 'Will you manage?'

James nodded and Willie let go his grip on the warps. He went forward along the waist by the wheelhouse. Spray was breaking over the starboard bow and driving across the deck. Below the wheelhouse Ian was bending over the ready-use locker. McPhail was standing beside him. He heard McPhail say, 'I was using them earlier. I think they're on the grab-rail down the port side.'

Ian straightened up and said, 'You bloody idiot! Can you not even put things back in their place?'

Willie shouted, 'Ian!' But the wind carried it away and Ian didn't hear. He was already following McPhail round the far side of the wheelhouse.

Willie went after them. He was at the corner of the wheel-house when he saw McPhail lift the wire-cutters from the grab-rail. He heard McPhail say 'Here!' in a lull in the wind. Ian took the cutters. They were shouting at each other now. Willie could not distinguish the words, because the wind took them and carried them out across the dark foam-flecked water astern. But he saw Ian raise the wire-cutters above his head. He saw McPhail wince and put up his hands to protect himself. He had no great love for McPhail. But there was murder in Ian's upraised arm and he yelled and launched him-self down the waist. His shoulder caught Ian as he half-turned and was off balance. Ian staggered against the gunwale, hung for a moment and went over backwards, shouting.

Willie clung to the gunwale and stared down in horror. At first he could see nothing but the broken water along the boat's side. Then a spread of yellow oilskin surfaced, already some way astern. McPhail pulled him away. Willie stared at him stupidly.

'He was going to murder you! My own brother!'

McPhail said, 'You go and tell the skipper. Tell him he's gone. But you saw nothing. Nothing! Remember that!'

Willie hesitated. McPhail said, 'You wouldn't want him to know, would you?'

Willie began, 'But Ian . . .'

McPhail said, 'Ian'll never come back, laddie. There's no chance. Give me a minute to get there first.'

He went forward, round the front of the wheelhouse, clutching the grab-rail.

James was still hanging on to the warps. James McColl was looking down from the wheelhouse window, as McPhail came round the forward end of the wheelhouse.

James said, 'I was shouting, Hughie. Did you not hear? Give me a hand with this.'

McPhail laid hold of the warps. Willie came round the after end of the wheelhouse, shouting.

'Ian's gone!'

James let go the warps and turned. 'Gone?'

'He must have gone over the side! There's no sign of him.'

James said to McPhail, 'Get this trawl cleared away somehow. Willie, get the men up from the hold.'

Then he went up to the wheelhouse. James McColl was at the RT.

James said, 'Ian's over the side.'

James McColl said, 'I know. I heard.' He handed James the microphone.

James said into it, 'James Campbell. *The Maid of Lorne.* Can any of you boys hear me? I'm in bad trouble . . .'

Sutherland was sitting on a radiator. Christine came out of the filing cupboard with the tea tray as Duthie was saying:

'We find that Ian Peter Campbell did, in the course of his employment as mate in the fishing vessel *The Maid of Lorne*, fall into the sea at about eight o'clock on the evening of fifteenth May and was drowned.'

Christine cleared a space at the corner of her desk and put the tray down.

'No blame?' asked Sutherland.

'No blame,' Duthie said. 'No negligence. No nothing.'

'It's possible that the Crown Office may want to raise the question of perjury.'

'Willie?'

'Yes. They may not, of course. In the circumstances.'

Duthie said, 'I hope not. He did come clean, poor kid. It was the Sheriff, of course.'

'There are no flies,' said Sutherland, 'on Archie Derwent . . . Thank you.'

He took a mug of tea from Christine. Duthie helped himself to a mug from the tray.

'All the same,' he said, 'I wish . . .'

'You wish you hadn't sought the truth quite so diligently.'

'I don't quite see what good it's done to anybody.'

Sutherland drank tea for a moment in silence.

'I was a medical student in 1939,' he said. 'When the war broke out there was the usual rash of enthusiasm to get into it and get it over, so I joined the infantry. I saw a lot of great work done by the medical people, patching up bodies, so that they could go back and get torn to pieces again. At the end of the war I felt that medicine wasn't quite what I wanted. I was still in the army, of course. When you were about five, I should think, I found myself at Nuremburg. Not in a legal capacity but as an infantry officer doing a certain job. I attended a good many of the trials. Most of the accused were deplorable people and got what they deserved. There was something missing, though. I didn't know what. But I thought, Justice! That's what the world needs now. I didn't realize at the time that I didn't quite know what justice was.'

'Do you know now?' Duthie asked.

Sutherland said, 'I know a little more about it. When I was

demobbed I went back to my university and read Law. Took an indifferent degree and joined a practice. I began to learn a little about the Fiscal Service, to which you and I now belong. It had one attraction to offset the modest remuneration, the hard work and the periods of boredom. Its function is the pursuit of justice. But more than in any other branch of the Law, its officers are permitted to exercise a great deal of compassion. And that's my point. I believe that justice without compassion is a fraud.'

He got up from the radiator on which he had been sitting and said to Christine, 'I think we might get Cairns to turn down the central heating a little. The weather's getting milder.'

V

Cairns turned off the central heating altogether as a mild spring turned into a warm summer overnight.

Duthie began to enjoy it. He had no great regard for the town itself. Its pattern of crime was mean rather than petty. It had a strongly defined hierarchy which he disliked, although by virtue of his office he belonged to one of its upper levels. For a town of its size there was a considerable amount of greed and corruption. There were hotel owners who were sharks, out for a quick buck, without much concern for the inn-keeping tradition. Some of the townspeople, as the tourists began to appear, reminded Duthie of small boys he had seen in Cairo (on a prolonged cruise which his father had given him as part of a liberal education) selling their little sisters.

But the air was good and the surrounding country magnificent. Christine had warmed and was pleasant and lively in the office. The Sheriff Clerk's eyes had lost their maternal expression. He had started to play golf again, had beaten Sutherland twice and been beaten once by the Sheriff, who gave him a bad time in court the following day in case the defeat had been diplomatic.

The work in the office was mainly routine. But a Dutch salvage crew working in the harbour – robust men with a taste for neat gin and women – enlivened the town for a week or two, until one of them died in an underwater accident. Then a young tinker girl was shot by her lover, who was discovered to belong to the very top level of the hierarchy, providing a pleasant fortnight for the gossips; but not for the girl, who lay on the edge of death in Glendoran hospital with an empty eye-socket and a ravaged face that had once been pretty.

It was on a pleasant day in mid-July that Duthie's cloud began to grow larger than a man's hand. On this day Angus McInnes was walking with his dog on the high ground above his house. He had received a letter that morning which he had pushed carelessly into a pocket until such time as he found the spectacles he had mislaid the previous evening. At the top of the high ground he sat down on a rock to fill a pipe. The letter came out with his tobacco pouch and lay in the heather beside the rock for a fortnight, until a day of heavy rain disintegrated it. It would not have troubled him much if he had known about it, but he never did. When his pipe was going he sat for a time watching the play of sunlight and cloud-shadow on the mainland. A patch of light hit the Bruaich, whose other name he still could not remember, and for a time the mountain looked almost serene. Then the light moved on. He followed it across the lesser hills, until it touched the soft green slopes above Ruigh. He did not know Ruigh, except as a name.

Ruigh had been farmed by the Lithgows for four generations. The first had made little of it. The second had put a hardy breed of sheep on it. The third, Hector Lithgow, who knew about sheep and had a good head for business, had improved the breed and enlarged Ruigh to about two thousand acres of hill pasture. The younger son of the fourth generation, Callum Lithgow, knew a great deal about sheep and had a very good head for business. He gradually assumed the management of Ruigh during his father's declining years, and at the time of Hector's death the Ruigh sheep were considered notable in places as far away as New Zealand. The elder son, Hamish, disliked sheep as much as he disliked his father, which was mutual, and went wandering in his late teens. He was a compulsive wanderer. He went into the merchant navy as a seaman and left it a year later at Brisbane. He bummed his way across Australia and stevedored for a time in Sydney. Some time later he was in British Columbia working on the Peace River project. When he got news of his father's death he had found sufficient gold in the Fraser River to take him back to Ruigh, comfortably but without a fortune. He planned eventually to return to British Columbia, for he had learnt one thing about it. With money to invest, it was wide open.

He was warmly welcomed at Ruigh. In spite of the differences between them in character, Callum had always had an affectionate relationship with his brother. Callum's wife, meeting her large, amiable brother-in-law for the first time, liked him. They would have been happy to have him settle permanently at Ruigh. He was entitled to, anyhow; for Hector, with some magnanimity, had divided his estate equally between them.

For a time it seemed that Hamish found the idea agreeable. Ruigh was certainly a pleasant place to live. But after a few months he began to show signs of restlessness again. He talked vaguely about taking a share out of the property and returning to Canada: a third only, which was generous, since technically a half of it was his. But he put no great pressure on Callum. It was only a suggestion. It came up again once or twice, and they talked around it, still vaguely. On the last occasion, however, Hamish found that his brother was getting a little bit hot under the collar about it, quoting figures which Hamish could not understand, and had no desire to anyhow. He had no inclination to get into an argument, so he changed the subject. He had been up on the high ground earlier that day, and had seen the Bruaich. As youths they had climbed on most of the mountains within reasonable reach, but the Bruaich had always given them the best sport. Hamish had a fancy to try it again: the Tower route preferably. Callum was doubtful at first. He had climbed occasionally in the past two years, once or twice on the Bruaich, when time permitted. Hamish probably had not climbed at all; and the Tower route was no place for a man out of condition. At the same time, the idea appealed to him. They had climbed well together in the past.

But Ruigh came first, of course. For Callum, Ruigh came before anything else, with the possible exception of his wife, of whom he was extremely fond. And this was a busy time. It would be a month at least before an expedition to the Bruaich could be contemplated.

That would have the advantage, however, of delaying any decision about Hamish going off on his wanderings again. So he agreed; and they got out the six inch map and began to talk about routes and methods and hazards. It took them back to their young days, before Hamish had been bitten by restlessness and Callum by his sheep.

Sutherland sat at his desk signing letters. Christine handed them to him one by one, and he read, signed and laid them aside.

'I'm going over to the other side to take precognitions this afternoon,' he said without interrupting the rhythm. 'I'll get the one o'clock boat. Is there anything before I go?'

'No,' she said. 'I don't think so. Back this evening?'

'Yes. I'll have to get the morning train if I'm to be in time for that damned dinner. One more or less has to pack in with burros to get to St Andrews since they removed the railways in that part of the world.'

'Then London?'

'Yes. It'll be about a week altogether. Did you get hold of Mr Campbell?'

'I called his office,' Christine said, 'but he hadn't come in. I expect he'll call back.'

'If he does, tell him it's not urgent.'

'All right.'

Sutherland signed the last of the letters and looked up.

'That's the lot?'

'Yes.'

'Good. It's time we had a new typewriter. This one's getting a bit superannuated.'

Christine said, 'It's a cow. Any chance of getting an electric?'

Sutherland smiled. 'You're an optimist. But I'll see what can be done.'

Christine said, as she went towards the door, 'It would make life a lot easier.'

'I had the impression,' Sutherland said, 'that Mr Duthie's arrival had made life a little easier for both of us.'

'It has,' she said seriously. 'It's quite pleasant having him around.'

Sutherland smiled, and she went out. That girl, he thought, is practically impregnable, but not quite. The ideal secretary. He settled down to the papers on the desk in front of him.

Christine was sorting out the letters at her desk when she heard the outside door open. She looked up, saw the County Clerk and gave him a bright smile.

'Hello, Mr Campbell. We were just talking about you. You'd like to see Mr Sutherland?'

'Thank you,' he said, without returning her smile. He seldom smiled, unless it was necessary.

Christine went to Sutherland's door, knocked, opened it and said, 'The County Clerk, Mr Sutherland.'

She stood aside for Campbell to go through and pulled the door shut after him.

Sutherland rose as Campbell came in and waved at a chair.

'Good morning, George. You shouldn't have bothered. There's nothing urgent about this.'

Campbell sat down. 'I had to come out anyhow. I thought I'd save a telephone call.'

Sutherland rummaged until he found what he wanted. 'I'm not quite clear about this thing you sent me . . . Yes, this is it.' He had found a file. He opened it and glanced through the contents for a moment. Then he added, 'Relating to Angus McInnes.'

Campbell said, 'It will be a prosecution under the Town and Country Planning (Scotland) Act, 1972.'

Sutherland looked up briefly and said, 'Will it?' There was a touch of asperity in his voice, which Campbell failed to notice. He looked down at the file again and went on, 'I'm a little rusty about this sort of thing. It doesn't often come our way. Would you care to enlighten me? Who is Angus McInnes?'

'Formerly a crofter. Now retired. Wife deceased.'

'And he's built himself a house without getting planning permission. Right?'

Campbell said, 'It appears that he bought a piece of land on which to build a house for his retirement. It came to our notice about two months ago that the house had been built without reference to my Planning Department.'

'Where is this piece of land?'

'At Camas Dearg, just where the McAllister land marches with the Glengarve estate.'

Sutherland got up and went over to the wall map. He traced Camas Dearg, after a search down the coastline with a finger.

'It's miles from anywhere,' he said. 'If the building's sound, surely planning permission's a formality.'

'It should have been obtained all the same. There might be objections.'

Sutherland snorted. 'From whom? The sheep? Or the deer?' He returned to his desk.

Campbell said, 'It's adjacent to the Glengarve estate.'

'Why should Sir Willie complain? It won't spoil his view.'

'Nevertheless, application should have been made.'

Sutherland gave an almost imperceptible sigh.

'All right. A couple of months ago your Planning Department discovered that the house had been built. What then?'

'We sent McInnes a letter asking him to submit an application on Form D1. Which he ignored. If people just wouldn't ignore correspondence . . .'

'There are people who don't enjoy writing letters,' Sutherland said. 'If he had applied? Would permission still have been granted?'

'That's hypothetical. He didn't. So a further letter was sent, requiring a reply within seven days.'

'Which wasn't forthcoming, I take it.'

'No. So the matter was then passed to me for action and I sent him an enforcement notice.'

'Enforcing what?'

'The removal of the building. It gave him twenty-eight days to appeal to the Secretary of State. That period of grace has now elapsed.'

'This notice has the force of law under the Act, of course?'

'Yes.'

Sutherland pondered. Then he said, 'Are you sure he received these communications? Were they sent by hand?'

'The enforcement notice was sent by registered mail. It was received all right.'

'Is it not customary to send your enforcement officer with a communication like that?'

'Occasionally. But it would have taken him a day to get to Camas Dearg and back, and in this case it seemed a waste of time.'

'Are you sure it was understood?'

Campbell said a little tartly, 'Its terms are clear enough. Why should it not be understood?'

'Are you sure, for instance, that McInnes could read it? Suppose he'd broken his spectacles?'

Campbell allowed himself a slightly wintry smile.

'I'm surprised at you, Fiscal. Here's a man that's clearly broken the law – I admit on a technicality. But broken it he has. I simply haven't the time to go into the ins and outs of the case, the humanitarian aspects.'

'That's a pity.'

Campbell shrugged. 'They'll come out in due course in the court, I've no doubt.' He looked at Sutherland curiously. 'You seem to be defending him, though you know as little about him as I do. I'd be interested to know why.'

'I can't tell you why,' Sutherland said. 'And I'm not exactly defending him. I'm just uneasy about it.'

He brooded over the file again for a few moments and then looked up.

'All right. What d'you want me to do?'

'Have him into court. Get a direction from the Sheriff to comply with the enforcement order.'

'And pull down his house?'

'I'm afraid there's no alternative. He'd twenty-eight days to appeal.'

Sutherland said, 'An old man who'd worked with his hands all his days. Living alone in retirement, miles from anywhere. Invited to pull down his house or appeal to no less a person than Her Majesty's Secretary of State for Scotland. For God's sake, George! It must have seemed a fearful proposition.'

Campbell shrugged again and said nothing. Sutherland rose.

'All right,' he said, 'I'll give some thought to it.'

'It requires more than thought, Fiscal.'

'A little preliminary thought can sometimes be of value,' Sutherland said. 'You may recall what happened to the Gadarene swine.'

Campbell stared at Sutherland, decided to make no comment and got to his feet.

Sutherland said, 'There's just one thing. This house has been built in a remote area. Nothing but hill grazing and grouse moor around it. How did you come to know about it?'

'We have ways and means, Fiscal,' Campbell said a little primly. 'I'm afraid my Planning Department would regard that as confidential.'

'Your Planning Department will give me whatever information I require, George,' Sutherland said gently. 'If it wants me to take any action.'

After a moment, Campbell said, 'We had our attention drawn to it by Sir William McWhirter of Glengarve.'

'You surprise me. I didn't think Sir Willie was like that.'

Campbell gave him another bleak smile and said, 'You've misjudged him, it seems.'

Sutherland opened the door for him. When Campbell had gone Sutherland looked at his watch and was surprised by the lateness of the hour. He returned to his desk, put some papers into a briefcase, picked up the McInnes file and went out to the main office.

Christine said, 'You haven't much time for lunch. Will I get you a sandwich?'

'I'll have something on the boat.' He gave her the McInnes

file. 'Put that on Mr Duthie's desk. I'll talk to him about it before I leave in the morning.'

Christine nodded and Sutherland went out.

The boats that sailed to the Islands from the Railway Pier covered a hundred miles or so on their voyage to the remoter parts of the Hebrides, calling at a number of small ports and harbours on the way. They passed through some of the most beautiful waters in the world, and in bad weather some of the most turbulent. This day was fine. Sutherland had a Guinness and a sandwich in the bar before the boat sailed, then went up on to the top deck to take the air, go through the papers in his briefcase and watch the scenery. He knew the scene by heart, all the islands, firths and bays, and the surrounding mountains; at all seasons of the year; in all kinds of weather from the winter gales to limpid summer days like this; and it never failed to delight him.

He was on the point of opening his briefcase, reluctantly, when McWhirter spoke behind him.

'Playing truant, John?'

Sutherland looked round. 'Hello, Willie. Unfortunately, no. I'm going over to precognosce a somewhat messy case of rape.'

'I suppose they have to do something to pass the time. Mind if I join you?' He had a glass in his hand.

Sutherland said, 'Please do,' and McWhirter sat beside him on the bench.

'I've a bone to pick with you anyhow,' Sutherland said.

McWhirter raised an eyebrow. 'What have I done?'

'You've got one of your neighbours into hot water.'

'*I* have?'

'McInnes is going to have to pull down his house. Or pay a daily fine until he does so.'

'That's not exactly what I intended. Pringle's a fool.'

'What did you intend?'

'I told my lawyer . . . you know Pringle?'

'It's hardly as warm a relationship as that,' Sutherland said dryly. 'I'm acquainted with him.'

76

McWhirter said, 'I told him to make sure we didn't have a rash of holiday chalets along the march fence. McAllister's a go-ahead sort of chap and tourists are fair game these days. I thought that's what might be happening when I first saw the thing.'

'When did you first see it?'

'I was on the hill with my keeper looking at the grouse. They're good this year, John. We saw this place and went down and talked to the old man.'

'Were you reassured after that?'

'To a certain extent.'

'Then why did you put Pringle on to it?'

McWhirter thought for a moment and then said, 'Temper, I suppose. If he hadn't shot at us I'd probably have gone home and cooled off and done nothing about it. For the time being, anyhow. I felt such a damn fool lying face down in the heather.'

Sutherland contemplated him for a moment in silence.

'Did you say he shot at you?'

'Well, not precisely at us.'

Sutherland waited. 'It makes a difference, you know,' he said after a moment.

McWhirter said, 'I suppose he just fired in the air. If a shotgun's fired in your direction you can hear the pellets in the heather. I've heard them often enough. There's always the occasional idiot out with the guns on a grouse shoot.'

'Did he threaten you with a gun?'

'No, no. Nothing like that at all. He was just letting off a bit of steam. My fault. I was sharp with him.'

'How did your keeper react?'

'Swore a couple of times in the Gaelic and then started to laugh. I think he enjoyed seeing me trying to present a low profile . . . Look here, I don't want to get McInnes into unnecessary trouble.'

'It depends what you mean by that. He's been sent a number of letters and a statutory notice. All of which he ignored.'

'He wouldn't understand them. He doesn't speak English. McGuffie had to translate from the Gaelic.'

'No excuse. He could always have had them translated.'

'Keep him out of trouble, John. No fines or anything like that.'

'I'll be away myself for a few days,' Sutherland said. 'But I'll have a word with Duthie, my depute. He can sit on it till I come back.'

They sat in silence for a time. The firth was like a mill pond. The only sounds were the remote throb of the engines, the soft wash of the water and the seagulls. There was very little sense of movement.

'At the same time,' McWhirter said, 'I don't really want anyone building quite so near my land.'

Sutherland looked round at him. 'You'll have to make up your mind what you do want.'

'It's a valuable grouse moor, John.'

'One old man and one small house won't affect that, surely.'

'It's a start. When he dies the land will pass, presumably, to somebody else. Who may get ideas about developing it.'

'There's nothing I can do about that. If you're concerned, I suppose you could bring a civil action.'

'For what?'

'I don't know, off-hand. To prevent development, I suppose. Assuming that the County Clerk and his Planning Department don't succeed in settling the matter for you.'

McWhirter said, 'Thank you.'

Sutherland said a little irritably, 'Don't thank me. I'd prefer not to be involved, even to that extent.'

'I'll speak to Pringle, anyhow. I'm sure there are better places for McInnes to build. Less isolated. After all, he's an old man. I'd be glad to help. Financially. To a reasonable extent.'

Sutherland laughed. McWhirter looked at him in surprise.

'What's funny about that?'

'Nothing at all,' said Sutherland. 'It's just a familiar pattern in this part of the world. The laird who spent most of his life elsewhere. The agent who took care of things in his absence. In the old days when they wanted the land cleared they burned down the houses over the heads of the occupants, in the alleged belief that Canada or Australia had more to offer them.'

McWhirter gave him a long, hard stare. 'You're not very kind, John.'

'Pay no attention to me,' Sutherland said. 'I'm not suggesting that you intend to have him burnt out. For an industrial giant, Willie, you're a very civilized man.'

Duthie sat with his chair tilted back and his feet up on a corner of the desk, reading the McInnes file. He made a note or two, thought about it for a little, then got up and went out into the main office. Christine was at her desk.

Duthie asked, 'Is the Old Man away yet?'

Christine said, 'Just getting ready. If you're going in, tell him he's going to miss his train.'

Duthie knocked on Sutherland's door and went in. Sutherland was repacking an open suitcase on his desk.

'Christine says you're going to miss your train,' Duthie said.

'She's been here long enough to know that trains from Glendoran never depart at the scheduled time.'

'This thing about Angus McInnes. She said you wanted to talk about it before you left.'

'Have you looked at it?'

'Yes. It seems clear enough. He's in breach of the Act, all right.'

Sutherland half emptied his suitcase and began again.

'Sit on it, all the same,' he said. 'You know Campbell. He's a great man for the small print. He'll have this poor old chap pulling down his house and then applying on Form whatever it is to build it again.'

'He's got the law on his side.'

'There's no harm been done. There's no dangerous precedent been set.'

Duthie looked troubled. 'I can't quite see how to get round it.'

Sutherland said, 'We may have to bring him into court, if only to keep Campbell happy. But we can find extenuating circumstances. McInnes doesn't seem to have the English for one thing. I'm sure if you were to put it to the Sheriff with your silver tongue he'd allow more time for the application. Let him beat you at golf again.'

79

'I didn't!' Duthie said indignantly. 'I'd do a lot of things, but not that.'

'You beat me, didn't you?'

'Yes. But that's different.'

'It's not different at all. I regularly beat Archie Derwent. Five and four, as a rule. Do some arithmetic.'

Duthie said, 'I was off my game. Why are you so interested in McInnes?'

Sutherland said, 'You and I may be old men ourselves one day.' He closed his suitcase. 'Is there anything else before I catch the train for which I am now seven minutes late?'

'I don't think so.'

'Good ... By the way, McInnes may be the subject of a civil action.'

'Who's bringing it?'

'Willie McWhirter.' He picked up his suitcase and moved towards the door. 'If Pringle issues a summons he'd better not send it through the mail.'

He went out into the main office, and Duthie followed.

'Otherwise,' Sutherland said, 'it'll go the way of all the others. I suspect under a tea caddy on the mantelpiece. That's the usual place.'

'Then McInnes would really be in the soup.'

'It might be a good idea if Pringle got a discreet hint to use a Sheriff Officer. With an interpreter. I should think the Sheriff Clerk could drop that into his ear.'

'I'll ask her.'

'What was all that about?' Christine asked, when Sutherland had gone.

'A mole hill,' said Duthie, 'just a mole hill. See for yourself.'

He laid the McInnes file on her desk.

Angus had done more work about the house. There was a small spread of gravel from the shore in front of the doorway, enclosed by a low rustic fence of larch. It set the place off nicely. Larch was a fine, lasting wood, and the dark grey bark blended nicely with the outcrops of rock and the dark green of the gorse.

The dog was asleep against the wall of the house. The old twelve-bore was propped near the door. Angus was sitting on the bench feeding scraps of bread to a number of small birds and talking to them softly in the Gaelic. It was another warm and gentle day.

The dog heard the men first and wakened suddenly. The birds scattered. Then Angus heard the voices in the distance and got to his feet.

There were two of them, walking along the track through the heather that slanted up towards the cottage. Fletcher, a Sheriff Officer, was a brisk, burly man without sentiment, who made an adequate living out of the problems of others. The smaller man was McPhee, a clerk in Fletcher's office, here because of his knowledge of Gaelic, which he was learning at night classes and spoke rather badly. He was not a remarkable personality and was completely dominated by Fletcher, whose simple desire at the moment was to get his business done as quickly as possible and get back to the mainland. It was too warm a day for the kind of walking they had had to do and Fletcher was overheated and irritable.

The collie was growling as they came up the last part of the track. Angus quietened it with a word in the Gaelic and waited, watching the men warily. As they approached he greeted them politely in the Gaelic.

Fletcher said, 'Are you Angus McInnes?'

McPhee said, '*An sibh-se 'n Aoghnas Mac-an-Aoghnais?*'

Angus said, '*Co eile bha thu 'n duil a bh'ann?*'

'He says, who else would he be?' McPhee said, looking at Fletcher.

'I'll take that as an affirmative,' Fletcher said, and reached into an inside pocket. He brought out a folded document with the dexterity of long practice and held it out to Angus, who looked at it curiously but made no effort to take it.

'This is a summons,' Fletcher said, 'to appear at the Sheriff Court at Glendoran. If you can't read it, my clerk will read it to you in the Gaelic.'

Angus looked questioningly at McPhee.

Fletcher handed the summons to McPhee and said, 'Here,

read it to him. Either it's quite true he's got no English or he's stupid.'

McPhee took the document, unfolded it and began to read, with some hesitation, in the Gaelic. ' '*Se* Sheriff Officer *a tha so summonadh airson gun teid sibh gu cuirt siorram Glendoran*.'

Angus waited politely until McPhee was out of breath and then made a brief remark which appeared to touch McPhee on a tender spot. McPhee answered hotly and at some length.

'What was that?' asked Fletcher suspiciously.

McPhee hesitated, and Fletcher demanded impatiently, 'What was it?'

'I said I can't help my accent. I've only had four sessions at the night school. I'm doing the best I can.'

'Never mind your accent. Just get on with it. As long as he understands.'

McPhee began to read again.

After a moment or two Angus interrupted him. '*Cuir air falbh am paipeir sin a bhalaich. Chan'eil mise 'G eisdeachd riut*,' he said, and turned away.

McPhee looked at Fletcher. 'He says put it away. He's not listening.'

'Tell him he'd better listen. Or he'll be in worse trouble than he is now.'

McPhee translated.

Angus said, '*Chan'eil mise an trioblaid 'sa bith*.'

'He says he's in no trouble,' said McPhee.

'Tell him he's in trouble, whether he thinks it or not,' said Fletcher irritably. 'He had no permission to build this house. He had a whole month to appeal to the Secretary of State for Scotland. Go on, tell him.'

McPhee began hesitantly and struggled on with mounting difficulty. Angus listened to him for the first time with interest, and when McPhee had stumbled to the end, he answered at some length. McPhee frowned and looked at Fletcher uneasily.

Fletcher said, 'Well?'

McPhee said, uncertainly, 'He says he didn't need the Secretary of State to help him build the house. He was able to do it himself.'

Fletcher wiped the sweat from his face with a handkerchief and said, 'Are you sure it's Gaelic you've been learning, McPhee? You haven't been learning Hindustani or something by mistake?'

McPhee took a deep breath and was about to answer with considerable heat; but Angus took the paper suddenly from his hand and threw it at Fletcher's feet. He spoke in the Gaelic for a moment, and McPhee translated.

'He says he has no need of your bit of paper and we can take it and get off his land.'

Fletcher said to Angus, 'You've been served with a summons.'

McPhee said, '*Fhuair sibh an Summonadh.*'

Angus turned his back on them and moved towards the house.

'Have it your own way,' said Fletcher. 'It won't do you any good . . . Come along, McPhee. We've wasted enough time.'

He turned and began to walk back down the track. McPhee followed him.

'You know,' said Fletcher, over his shoulder, 'there's some of them get so scared when you hand them a writ that they'll ask you in for a cup of tea. I suppose they think it might soften you up.'

'No such luck this time,' said McPhee.

The track ran through deep heather at this point, but a few yards off it there was a small grassy patch in which a hare was feeding. It was disturbed by the sound of their voices and stood up on its hind legs, ears twitching, looking around nervously. Angus had turned at the door of his house to watch the two men go off his land, and he caught the small movement of the hare out of the corner of his eye.

Fletcher and McPhee had been totally unaware of it.

'What time's the boat?' asked Fletcher, still over his shoulder.

'Half past three, Mr Fletcher.'

'We should make it easy enough.'

They were still unaware of the hare which was now on the run, dodging and leaping through the heather.

A shot rang out, not far away. McPhee stopped and half turned, mouth hanging open in astonishment. He was aware momentarily of Angus McInnes standing at his front door with a gun at his shoulder before Fletcher gripped his arm and shouted.

'Run, man, run! The old fool's gone off his head!'

They began to run. Fletcher drew slowly ahead; not because he was in better condition generally or had less courage, but because McPhee had a varicose vein, which troubled him on occasions like this.

Outside the door of his house, Angus watched the two running men with interest for a moment or two. Then he broke the twelve-bore, ejecting the two spent cartridges, spoke to the collie in Gaelic, and they began to walk down the hill together.

VI

'When did this happen?' Duthie asked. He was considerably perturbed. Sit on it, Sutherland had said. And now this.

'Yesterday afternoon,' said McKechnie. 'Fletcher went over with one of his men to serve a summons. You'll know about that, I think.'

'I knew it might happen. But not as quickly as this.'

'Anyhow,' said McKechnie, 'they got into a bit of an argument. You've met Fletcher. You may know what he's like – throws his weight around. And when they were leaving McInnes fired a couple of shots at them.'

They were in the main office: Christine at her desk, listening in silence; McKechnie sitting in one of the stiff office chairs with his cap on his knee; Duthie prowling and uneasy.

'Either of them hit?' he asked.

'No. But they were scared. They took to their heels. And Fletcher came raging in to us as soon as he got back. Wanted us to go over and arrest him on the spot. Deforcement of an officer, he said.'

'He should have had more sense.'

'I was inclined to agree with him. Is that not what it was?'

'Not nowadays. Aggravated assault. If anything ... You haven't seen McInnes yet?'

'I'm going over now. I'll take Constable Ross with me. He speaks a bit of Gaelic.'

'For God's sake be careful. Don't throw too many questions at him.'

McKechnie smiled and said, 'Don't worry, Mr Duthie. I'm not new at the business. We'll be circumspect.'

'I'm sorry,' Duthie said, and grinned. 'Teaching grandma to suck eggs. But he is a prime suspect.'

When McKechnie had left Christine said, 'Quite an active little mole.'

Duthie was lost and said so.

'I mean,' she said, 'it might turn out to be a big mole hill.'

The inside of the house was spartan but very clean and fresh. There was a scrubbed deal table and two kitchen chairs. There was a basket chair beside the open hearth designed to burn peat, and a basket of peats beside that. There was a dresser, of the Welsh dresser type, which Angus himself had made. There was some crockery set up on it, which his wife had picked up long ago at a sale in some big house. If McKechnie had known about such things he would have recognized it as early Minton. In one corner of the room there was a simple bed, covered now with a brightly coloured blanket.

There was no luxury; but for a man who had never known or desired luxury, there was great comfort. Outside, there was almost everything he required. Up on the high ground at the back, there was a bog that would outlive him as a source of peat. Below in a sheltered place he had started a vegetable patch. The question of a goat or a cow had still to be decided. Sufficient of his neighbours' game strayed into his property to ensure variety in the pot. There would be honey next year from the bees. When he had his boat the few things that he wanted from outside, like paraffin for the Tilley, would be easy enough to bring in. He made no demands on society. But he was contributing to it, for he was creating something.

He felt no animosity in the big sergeant who was moving quietly around the room, examining it, and admiring it too. The silence was neutral and not uncomfortable. The twelve-bore lay on the scrubbed table. No one had touched it except Angus himself, who had brought it down from its hooks on the wall when the young constable (whose Gaelic was a lot better than yon other fellow's) had asked him to.

Ross came in with two cartridge cases in his hand, spent but fresh in appearance, 'I found them outside. Just by the door,' he said.

McKechnie examined them, sniffed them.

Ross said, 'They won't have been lying around more than a day or two.'

'Ask him when he last used the gun.'

'*Cuin a loisg thu an gunna so mu dheireadh?*' Ross said to Angus.

'*An de. Marbh mi coinneanach.*'

'Yesterday,' said Ross. 'He shot a hare.'

'What time of day?'

Ross asked, got the answer, and grinned. 'He's no fool. Just after the two gentlemen left, he says. They were walking down the path when they flushed it out of the heather nearby.'

'Did the two gentlemen see it?'

Ross translated; then translated the reply. 'He doesn't think so. He says at about that time they began to run.'

'Has it occurred to him,' McKechnie asked, 'to wonder why they began to run?'

When Angus answered, Ross said, 'He thinks they were afraid they were going to miss the boat back to the mainland.'

'He's a cunning old devil. I'm wondering if he isn't too cunning. Where's this hare he shot?'

Ross asked Angus, who said, '*Dh' ith mi fhein 'san cu e.*'

Ross said, 'He and the dog ate it.'

'And burnt the fur and the bones, of course,' said McKechnie. 'No point in asking. Ask him if he'd let me borrow his gun for a few days.'

Ross did so. Angus hesitated. But native courtesy was strong in him and he said, '*O ceart gu leor.*'

'Okay,' said Ross.

McKechnie said, 'I'll give him a receipt for it. See if you can find any traces of the hare.'

He drew out a chair, sat at the table and began to write out a receipt. He checked the gun as he did so, for maker's name and details that might identify it.

Ross made a search in the likely places for the hare's remains but found nothing.

'Not a smell of it,' he said.

'Too bad,' said McKechnie.

He tore the page carefully from his note book and laid it on the table. He picked up the gun.

'Ask him if we'll be able to find him here during the next few days. If necessary.'

Ross did so, and Angus answered in the Gaelic, 'For longer than that, if God is willing.'

'I hope he's right,' said McKechnie. 'But there may be others that won't be.'

He nodded to Angus and went out with the gun.

Ross said in the Gaelic, 'Thank you for helping us, Mr McInnes.'

'*Se ur beatha,*' said Angus courteously.

When Ross had followed McKechnie out, Angus turned to the mantelpiece and found a pair of steel-rimmed spectacles. He picked up the receipt, examined it, then put it with other papers under the tea caddy. He put his spectacles back on the mantelpiece and looked at the dog, which had been lying quietly in a corner.

'I just hope they don't lose our gun, Linn,' he said in the Gaelic.

A document marked A REPORT FOR THE CONSIDERA-TION OF PROCEEDINGS lay on Duthie's desk. Duthie looked at it moodily. He lit himself a cigarette and pushed the packet across the desk to McKechnie, who was sitting on the other side, on one of the plastic-covered metal chairs.

'What kind of proceedings were you thinking about?' Duthie asked.

'That's up to you, Mr Duthie.'

'Breach of the peace? Reckless discharge of a firearm? Attempted murder? I mean, it depends what was in his mind, doesn't it?'

'Yes.'

'What was in his mind?'

'Dinner, I would think,' said McKechnie after a moment's thought. 'Difficult to say, though, with him speaking in Gaelic.'

'There was no trace at all of the hare?'

'None.'

'Are there any hares around that part?'

'Constable Ross and I raised two or three on the way back.'

'So that story could be true.'

'Oh, yes. It's quite possible. It's also possible that McInnes and the dog ate it.'

'He must have had a damn good appetite.'

'The open air life.'

'On the other hand,' Duthie said, 'he could have shot it some days ago. He's an old man. May have been a bit confused. Got his days mixed up. Very conveniently.'

'I don't think there's much wrong with his memory.'

'Anyhow, no corroboration. So it doesn't help.'

McKechnie sat frowning for a moment. 'Surely no sensible man would take a shot at a Sheriff Officer just because he'd delivered a summons? That's going a bit too far. He would have to be stupid or have a wicked temper.'

'Did he seem stupid to you?'

'Not in the least. And he showed no noticeable sign of temper.'

'He wouldn't with the police around. Unless he was stupid.'

'True enough.'

Duthie pulled the report towards him and leafed through it, brooding.

'No record, I suppose? Never done anything like this before?'

'Not that we know of.'

Duthie thought for a moment longer and then put the report to one side.

'Okay. I'll see Fletcher and his man. Then I'll let you know what we're going to do.'

'Right, Mr Duthie,' said McKechnie.

He got up and carefully replaced his chair against the wall with the other two.

The Sheriff Officer is not an officer of the Sheriff Court, or a Civil Servant like the Procurator Fiscal. His status in relation to the work of the Sheriff Court has been recognized by long use and tradition, but he is an individual running a business for profit, sometimes in a small partnership, sometimes in a larger firm. Fletcher was sole partner in a small firm. His name was on a frosted glass panel in a door at the top of a narrow flight of stairs covered with worn linoleum: 'J. Fletcher – Sheriff Officer and Messenger-at-Arms'.

An adenoidal girl with a tray on which a number of mugs slopped tea backed through the door and Fletcher's voice, loud and aggressive, became audible.

'It's not the first time a Sheriff Officer's been assaulted, Mr Duthie,' he was saying.

They were in an untidy room with nondescript furniture, filing cabinets, a desk littered with files and documents, a bentwood coatstand with a bowler hat and a raincoat on it, and an uncomfortable customer's chair on which Duthie was sitting. Fletcher was behind the desk.

'Not by any means,' he said. 'I've been kicked, punched, hit with sticks. I've had half bricks thrown at me. I've been barricaded out when I've gone to serve a summons or poind goods for an unpaid debt. You wouldn't credit the way people behave.'

The girl with the tray appeared in the half open doorway.

'And now,' said Fletcher, 'I've been shot at. Come in, Jessie. Will you partake of tea, Mr Duthie?'

'No, thank you.'

'I always have a cup at this time,' said Fletcher, and transferred a mug from the tray to his desk, where the rings left by its predecessors were still apparent. 'Shut the door behind you, Jessie. Is Mr McPhee back yet?'

'No, Mr Fletcher.'

'Tell him I want him in here as soon as he comes.'

The girl nodded and went out. The door closed behind her.

'You've never been shot at before?' asked Duthie.

'What's the difference? It's deforcement, Mr Duthie. It all comes to the same thing.'

'It wouldn't have come to the same thing if he'd hit you.'

Fletcher laughed. 'It's a good thing he's an old man, eh? And maybe not too good with his eyesight. But he came near enough all the same.'

'How near?'

'I could hear the shot whistling through the heather.'

'Are you sure he was firing at you?'

'Me or McPhee. Or both of us. We were close together.'

'How far away were you from McInnes?'

'We'd gone about fifty yards, maybe.'

'And McInnes was shooting from the front of his cottage?'

'That's right.'

'How d'you know? Did you see him?'

'No. But McPhee saw him.'

'He stopped to look, did he?'

'He kind of half turned. Then I called to him to run. I wasn't for taking any chances.'

There was a knock at the door.

Fletcher said, 'That'll be McPhee now ... Come in, McPhee!'

The door opened and McPhee came in.

'You can ask him yourself, Mr Duthie. Close the door, McPhee. You know Mr Duthie from the Fiscal's office.'

McPhee closed the door and nodded to Duthie.

Duthie said, 'You've had a harrowing experience, Mr McPhee.'

'It was that, Mr Duthie.'

'Mr Fletcher tells me you actually saw McInnes firing at you.'

McPhee hesitated, looked quickly at Fletcher, then back again at Duthie.

'Well, not exactly. I looked round when I heard the shot ...'

'You looked round? So you had no immediate reason to think that you might be the target?'

'I never thought at all. I just looked round. And there he was with the gun pointing. Then Mr Fletcher yelled and I turned and ran.'

'Where was the gun pointing?'

McPhee looked puzzled.

'It was pointing at us.'

'He was fifty yards away and you only got a brief look at him. But you're quite sure he was aiming at you.'

McPhee said, with a hint of indignation in his voice, 'Well, where else would he be aiming?'

'Ay, Mr Duthie,' said Fletcher, 'can you answer that?'

Duthie said, 'The police have examined this gun. It's interesting. Both barrels are full choke. This is a bit unusual. It suggests, for one thing, that McInnes is quite an expert with a twelve-bore.'

Fletcher looked at him suspiciously and said, 'What are you hinting at?'

'I'm not hinting at anything. I just think you'd have known all about it if he'd been shooting at you at fifty yards range.'

'You're suggesting that I'm lying.'

'No. I'm suggesting that McInnes may have been shooting at something else.'

'Then what was he shooting at? Tell me that. Was he just trying to put the fear of death into us or what? It was a damn dangerous thing to do anyhow. And it's still deforcement.'

Duthie said, 'It could have been a hare.'

Fletcher stared at him. 'Does he say that?'

'It's been suggested as a possibility.'

Fletcher grinned slowly. 'Don't you fall for that, Mr Duthie. Where's his corroboration?'

'Where's Mr McPhee's?'

'There's two of us, isn't there?'

'But you didn't look round,' Duthie said mildly. 'You didn't see what McInnes was doing. You just yelled and ran. I don't blame you. I'd probably have done exactly the same thing. But it's a pity, isn't it?'

Fletcher looked at Duthie in angry silence for a moment or

two. 'Are you going to proceed against him?' he asked at length.

'I don't know yet.'

'Let me tell you this,' Fletcher said, half on his feet, with his hands spread wide on the desk. 'My job's hard enough. If I can't get support from your office when I'm subjected to a violent assault, I'll ask for police protection every time I go out officially. Somebody's going to want to know why, Mr Duthie. And somebody's going to have to explain.'

Duthie got to his feet and said, still mildly, 'You're angry, Mr Fletcher.'

'Angry? I'm bloody angry. I'm as mad as a wet hen.'

'So I think we'll forget your last remark. My office isn't open to threats or pressure. You'll both be informed if we decide to proceed.'

Christine came in with some papers for Duthie's in-tray. Duthie was sitting with his chair tilted back, going through notes on this morning's court cases.

'You're going to be late,' Christine said. 'You're in court in five minutes.'

Duthie looked at his watch. 'It can't be that time.'

'It is.'

Duthie gathered up some papers from the desk in front of him and got to his feet. He went over to the coat rack for his gown and shrugged it on. Christine started to tidy his desk.

'Mr Pringle's in court this morning,' she said.

'That's why I forgot the time. It's called a Freudian block, or something. If not, it should be.'

'He wants to see you afterwards.'

'What about?'

'He didn't say. Probably Angus McInnes.'

'Ah. I forgot he was Sir Willie's man. Can't you put him off?'

'Not really. I think you'll have to see him. You'll be eyeball to eyeball with him in three minutes, anyhow.'

'A delicious prospect, at ten o'clock in the morning. Why are Fiscals obliged to sit opposite other lawyers? Why can't they sit opposite Sheriff Clerks?'

Christine said, 'I suppose you could, if you really wanted to. You could even sit beside her and hold hands. But then you'd have your back to the Sheriff and he might not like that.'

'We could sit with our backs to the dock, facing the Sheriff.'

'He might get confused and marry you. I wouldn't do that.'

Duthie grinned and said, 'You wouldn't. I might.'

Christine said, a little tartly this time, 'You have one minute.'

Duthie said, 'I'd better go.'

Christine turned from the desk. 'What are you going to do about him? The old man, I mean. McInnes.'

'I don't know yet. I can mark it "no proceedings". I can have him on a summary charge – breach of the peace or something. Or I can put out a petition warrant. But that makes it a big deal.'

'Well . . . which?'

Duthie was checking through the papers in his hand. 'Why does everybody want to know what I'm going to do about him? I don't know myself. I haven't had time. I've got to think.'

He went back to his desk and began to rummage through the papers Christine had just put in order, creating confusion again.

'Did you happen to see . . . Oh, here it is.'

'Did you see Fletcher?' Christine asked.

'Yes.'

He was rearranging the papers in his hand. She watched him until it was clear that he was going to say no more.

'I *am* interested,' she said.

Duthie got the papers the way he wanted them, then looked at her.

'Why?'

'Because I think I'd do the same thing myself if people kept pushing me around.'

'What did he do?'

'Always the legal beagle. What do *you* think he did?'

Duthie said, 'I think he shot a hare. But I think that mainly because Fletcher tried to threaten me, not because there's any evidence one way or the other. So I'm probably going to mark it "no proceedings".'

'There are times,' she said, 'when I hardly dislike you at all.'

93

Duthie grinned and said, 'How long have I got?'

She checked her watch again. 'You're one minute late. You'll have to run all the way.'

Duthie reached the landing outside the courtroom short of breath. A number of people were waiting: two or three police constables; small groups of slightly nervous individuals talking together in low voices, whom Cairns was trying to herd into the rooms marked WITNESSES – MALE and WITNESSES – FEMALE; and there was Pringle, talking to a youth with acne, presumably a client, too busy at the moment to notice Duthie. Liz Hamilton came out of the Sheriff's room, saw Duthie and gave him a bright smile.

'You needn't have hurried,' she said. 'The Sheriff's late.'

Duthie was still panting slightly. 'Thanks very much. What's happened to him?'

'He's had a flat tyre. I phoned Christine but you'd just left.'

She went on into the courtroom, and Duthie found Pringle at his elbow.

'Good morning, Mr Pringle,' he said.

Pringle nodded. 'This might give us an opportunity to begin our discussion on the McInnes matter. I'm concerned about it.'

'Naturally,' said Duthie. 'I understand the thing came up originally because of a complaint by Sir William.'

'That is correct.'

'Unfortunately, these things do take time. The Planning Department had to go through their customary exercises. We've now been asked to cite him for non-compliance. And that's the position at the moment.'

'That's not the aspect I'm talking about.'

'Surely it's the only aspect we can talk about?'

'I hope you're not deliberately evading the point, Mr Duthie. I refer to the assault on Mr Fletcher, the Sheriff Officer.'

'I'm afraid we can't discuss that. It's still under investigation.'

'An assault involving the discharge of firearms is a very serious matter,' Pringle said firmly. 'Time must not be wasted.'

'Nobody's wasting time, Mr Pringle,' said Duthie reassuringly. 'We're all grasping it firmly by the forelock.'

Pringle frowned. 'It's hardly an occasion for levity. As Sir William's legal adviser I would like to know what's happening.'

'You're not alone, Mr Pringle. Join the queue.'

Pringle frowned. 'I don't quite understand . . .'

Cairns said, as he passed, 'Sheriff's car's just arrived, Mr Duthie.'

Duthie thanked him and said to Pringle, 'Shall we go in and . . . join the lady?'

Pringle gave him a cold look. 'We'll take this up afterwards, Duthie.'

Christine looked up as McKechnie came in.

'You have a great instinct,' she said. 'I've just made it.'

McKechnie smiled and said, 'I'm looking for Mr Duthie, too.'

'He's still in court.' She looked at her watch. 'He shouldn't be long, if you want to wait.'

She went on with her work. McKechnie went into the filing cupboard. He came out again after a moment with two mugs of tea, and put one of them down beside her.

'Was there anything particular?' she asked.

'Nothing urgent. The Chief Inspector was wondering if he's decided what to do about McInnes.'

'Strictly off the record, he'll probably do nothing.'

'Well, maybe he's right.'

'Do you think so?'

McKechnie laughed. 'There are times when I think what I'm told to think, Christine. Nothing else.'

The outside door opened and Pringle came in, followed by Duthie. Duthie was still wearing his gown. Pringle had his over his arm. He crossed the office towards Sutherland's door.

'My room, Mr Pringle,' said Duthie abruptly. He pushed open his door and Pringle altered course and went through it.

Christine raised an eyebrow and pointed at her tea mug. Duthie shook his head and said something with his lips, silently. She thought about it and decided that it was 'Not bloody likely.'

Duthie pulled out one of the plastic-covered metal chairs and slid it across the floor towards his desk.

'Make yourself comfortable,' he said.

Pringle sat down carefully.

'You surprise me, Duthie,' he said. 'Indeed, you astonish me. You seriously mean you're not going to charge the man?'

Duthie was at the coat rack, getting rid of his gown.

'There's no corroboration,' he said.

Pringle twisted round in his chair and looked at him curiously.

'No corroboration?'

Duthie moved round to his desk. Christine had left some letters on it. As he looked through them, Duthie said, 'Well, there's a certain amount of corroboration by fact and circumstance. The gun was fired. There were two spent cartridge cases. McInnes admits he discharged the gun at about the time Fletcher was there. But not against Fletcher. And nobody claims to have actually seen him do so.'

Pringle waited. 'Nothing else?'

'No.'

'Nothing else that seems to you to be relevant?'

'No. So I don't think there's much of a case.'

'A second discharge of firearms,' said Pringle, 'within a short period of time and in precisely similar circumstances. And you think there's not much of a case?'

Duthie, who had been about to sit down, remained on his feet and stared at Pringle.

'Second?'

'Yes.'

'When was the first?'

'Didn't you know that he fired at Sir William?'

'No, I didn't.'

Duthie sat down slowly.

Pringle said, 'I'd have thought Mr Sutherland would have mentioned it.'

He was enjoying this. He watched Duthie trying to sort it out.

96

Duthie said, 'I don't suppose he knew.'

'I'm sure he did. In fact, he discussed it with Sir William.'

'Then why didn't he tell me?'

Pringle laughed. 'You seem to be out of step. Listening to different drummers, no doubt.'

Duthie sat forward and shuffled through the papers on his desk, to give himself a moment to get over his irritation.

'When did this happen?' he asked at length.

'When Sir William first remonstrated with McInnes about the cottage. Sir William and his head keeper, McGuffie, were leaving when two shots were fired.'

'Fired at them?'

'Both Sir William and McGuffie very naturally took cover. They didn't actually see the firing of the shots. A precisely similar situation, you'll agree.'

Duthie said nothing. Pringle tilted his metal chair back carefully and clasped his hands over his abdomen.

'I would have said,' he remarked, 'that the significance of this could hardly escape even the most partisan observer.'

Duthie said angrily, 'Look, Mr Pringle, I have no personal interest . . .'

Pringle interrupted him quickly. 'I'm not suggesting that you're grinding any axes, Duthie. Not in the least. But to the outsider it might seem that you're being a bit . . . what shall I say? . . . leisurely. Not knowing, of course, that there had been a certain lack of communication within your office.'

'Why didn't Sir William make a complaint at the time?' Duthie asked.

'I urged him to. I urged him very strongly. But he's a kindly man. He didn't want to make trouble.'

'I'd like to talk to him. Is he at home just now?'

'Unfortunately, he's in New York.'

'When does he get back?'

'In about ten days.'

Duthie pondered. Pringle contemplated him shrewdly.

'You'll have to do something before that, I'm afraid. Before we have the place littered with corpses.'

'Don't be absurd. Anyhow, the police have got his gun.'

97

Pringle smiled. 'A figure of speech, Duthie. But it's a serious matter.'

'I'm aware of that.'

'The Sheriff Officer was serving a summons on my behalf in a civil action when he was subjected to a violent assault. That is how I see it.'

'I accept that,' said Duthie.

'You'll have to do more than accept it. Or I'll feel obliged to put it to the Crown Office.'

'All right. I'll have him in on a summary charge. I don't quite know yet how I'll frame it.'

Pringle said, 'A summary charge is for minor offences, surely. The everyday peccadillo. Do you include the reckless discharge of firearms in that category?'

Duthie decided to end the interview and got to his feet.

'That's my problem,' he said.

'To the danger of the lieges?' said Pringle. 'With intent to do grievous bodily harm? You'll have to think about it very carefully.'

'I'm obliged to you for telling me about this.'

Pringle said, 'I regard it as my duty.'

He let his chair down carefully and stood up. Duthie came round his desk and opened the door.

'I really thought the Fiscal would have discussed it with you,' Pringle said. 'That's why I found your attitude hard to understand at first . . .'

'I can see that,' said Duthie. 'Thank you for letting me know.'

'I'm always glad to help, Duthie,' Pringle said kindly, and went out.

Duthie returned to his desk and sat down. He stared at the papers in front of him and took a number of deep breaths.

Christine looked at her watch. 'I'll just remind him you're here,' she said. 'I expect Pringle's put him to sleep.'

She was on her feet when the door of Duthie's room opened suddenly.

'The sergeant was wondering . . .' she began.

Duthie said, 'Is that tea fresh?'

'Yes. Fairly.'

Duthie went into the filing cupboard.

Christine said, 'Fresh enough, anyhow.'

After a moment Duthie came out with a mug in his hand. He looked at McKechnie.

'Did you know that McInnes discharged a shotgun at Sir William McWhirter? At. In the direction of. Or in the presence of.'

McKechnie stared at him. 'No. I did not.'

'Well, he did. According to Pringle.'

'Go on!'

'It makes a difference.'

'Yes. I would say it does. But it would depend a bit on the circumstances.'

'We won't know the circumstances for ten days. And we can't wait that long.'

'No. I don't suppose so.'

Duthie thought for a moment, then came to a decision.

'You'd better tell the Chief Inspector it'll be a petition warrant.'

McKechnie shrugged very slightly and said, 'Very good, Mr Duthie.'

He picked up his cap and went out.

Christine went on with her work for a little. Then she stopped and looked at Duthie. Her face was troubled.

'Homer seems to have nodded,' she said.

'Who?'

'Or whoever it was. He's slipped, hasn't he? Or didn't he know?'

'Didn't who know?'

'Mr Sutherland,' she said.

'He knew.'

She watched him for a moment; and she knew that he was troubled too, and liked him for it.

'Will it make a big difference?'

'For McInnes? Yes.'

'But it could still have been a hare . . . couldn't it?'

'I think it was. But nobody's going to believe it now.'

'Then I wish he'd done the job properly,' she said, 'and got some fun out of it. I don't much care for Fletcher.'

Duthie looked shocked.

'That's a very unprofessional remark.'

'I've got a very unprofessional side to my character,' Christine said. 'I don't often get a chance of revealing it.'

VII

Sutherland arrived back by the morning train. He stopped at the station bookstall to buy the Glendoran weekly newspaper, so that he could bring himself up to date with the local news and gossip, then walked to the office.

It was less enjoyable than on the last occasion. Even at this hour the pavements were crowded and the car traffic was heavy and sluggish in the bottlenecks of the narrow streets. The town was coming up to the peak of its tourist season.

Returning to it was no pleasure as it once had been. The air was no longer as stimulating, though it was certainly better than in the south and it got the blood flowing again. It had nothing to do with age, because physically he was still very fit. Maybe it was time to leave the Fiscal Service, spend a few dull years in property, make a bit of money before it was too late, and live in another country, away from remembered places.

Christine was removing the cover from her typewriter when he came in.

'Hello!' she said. 'You're early.'

'The train was on time, if that's what you mean. Duthie in yet?'

'Not yet. The mail's on your desk. I'll bring some tea in.'

'Thank you.'

He went into his room and put down his suitcase. He leafed through a neat stack of opened letters on his desk, decided to leave them till later and pushed them out of sight. He sat down and spread out the Glendoran paper. He scanned it casually at first, and then with sudden attention as he saw the headline. CROFTER ON SHOTGUN CHARGE. He read with concentration, frowning; then he got up suddenly, gathered up the paper and went rapidly through to the main office.

Christine was coming out of the filing cupboard with the tea tray.

'What in Heaven's name has Duthie been playing at?' Sutherland demanded.

She was startled by his violence. He held up the paper so that she could see the headline.

'Oh, yes,' she said. 'About McInnes.'

'I know it's about McInnes. I can read. What happened?'

'You'd better ask Mr Duthie.'

'I'm asking you.'

She hesitated. 'Well, McInnes says he just shot a hare . . .'

'But he's on a petition warrant,' Sutherland said harshly. 'Was that necessary? You know what it means?'

Christine said, 'Look, it's not my job. Don't bawl me out.'

'I'm sorry,' Sutherland said, more quietly. 'Get me the file, please.'

She laid the tea tray on the desk, went to a filing cabinet, brought out a file and handed it to Sutherland. He stood in the middle of the room, reading it. She put his mug of tea on the corner of the desk beside him and sat down. Sutherland went through the papers in the file in silence and drank tea intermittently.

The outer door opened and Duthie came in. He stopped as he saw Sutherland and looked quickly at Christine. She shrugged slightly.

'Morning,' said Duthie.

Sutherland looked up briefly, then continued reading.

Duthie went into the filing cupboard and came out after a moment or two with a mug of tea.

Sutherland closed the file, laid it on Christine's desk and said, 'Why a petition warrant?'

Duthie said, 'I'd no option.'

'There's always room for discretion.'

'There's not much room for discretion when a silly old man goes around firing shotguns at people.'

'You don't find Fletcher's story implausible?'

'I got the impression he believed what he told me. Whether he was mistaken or not.'

'You don't find it implausible that even a hot-tempered old man who believed he was being persecuted would bring inevitable disaster upon himself by deliberately shooting at an officer of the law?'

'He shot very close to them, anyhow.'

'You don't find it plausible that he was shooting at a hare?'

'It's quite possible,' said Duthie. 'But it was a damned careless thing to do.'

He laid his tea mug on the tray and put sugar and milk into it, as much as anything else to let his anger cool down, for he was very angry.

Sutherland said, 'There are degrees of recklessness.'

'Yes.'

'You remember the case of Niven, 1795 I think it was? He fired a cannon up a lane and claimed in his defence that he hadn't meant to do anybody any harm. He didn't get away with it. But that's a different matter, I think you'll agree.'

'Yes.'

'McInnes had a twelve-bore which he knew how to handle, not a cannon. And he didn't fire up a lane. He'd a few thousand acres of grouse moor around him. He may have been over-confident. But not necessarily reckless.'

'Unfortunately,' Duthie said, 'he was making a habit of it.'

Sutherland looked surprised. 'What d'you mean?'

Duthie exploded. 'Why the hell didn't you tell me he shot at Sir William McWhirter?'

'Because I forgot. Because you and my secretary were bundling me into a train that didn't leave until ten minutes after I got to it.'

'It made things damned awkward for me.'

'I don't see why. It was irrelevant.'

Duthie stared. 'Irrelevant?'

'He didn't shoot at Sir Willie McWhirter. He fired in the air. He was letting off steam. He was fingering his nose at bureaucracy.'

'Is that what he said?'

'It's what Sir Willie said. He was perfectly clear about it. There was no threat. No gun was fired in his direction. He had no complaint at all.'

'That's not Pringle's story.'

'For God's sake, Duthie! Pringle's a bumbling nonentity. No doubt with good intentions. It's a dangerous combination. You should know what he's like by now.'

Duthie said, 'I'm sorry. But he seemed to know what he was talking about.'

'He's made a fool of you,' Sutherland said bluntly. 'That doesn't matter. It doesn't do any of us any harm from time to time. But he's made a scapegoat of an old man who just wanted to be left in peace. And that is tragic.'

'Well, why didn't you tell me about it? You didn't have to behave like Pontius bloody Pilate!'

Sutherland stared at him in silence; and after a moment Duthie said more calmly, 'What else could I have done?'

'I'm sorry,' Sutherland said. 'You're quite right. I'm afraid I brushed it under the rug.'

'I suppose I could have made it a summary charge,' Duthie said. 'And damn Pringle.'

'It would have been better. The Sheriff knows this part of the country. He knows that hares get shot at. It's a family affair, in a way. It should have been fought out on our own doorstep.'

Christine said, 'Will it not be? I mean, what's the difference?'

Sutherland looked at her as though he had forgotten she was there.

'With a petition warrant,' he said, 'the details must be reported to Edinburgh. They're less interested in hares. But they know that Sheriff Officers are often subjected to violence. They'll take a different point of view.'

'It doesn't follow . . .' Duthie began uneasily.

'No, it doesn't follow,' said Sutherland. 'But it's just possible that this will become a serious charge in the High Court.'

Iain Cameron stood at the picture window in the coffee lounge looking through the big brass telescope on a tripod. The Lairig Hotel had been a coaching inn for two hundred years when he bought it close on thirty years ago. It was used mainly by climbers at that time. He had modernized it discreetly, retaining the old-fashioned atmosphere but adding a touch of sophistication, and now it was filled with tourists in the summer, the skiing crowd in the winter, and the climbers at all seasons of the year. The hotel stood in a green, heathery strath beside a brisk trout stream. There were mountains all around it, but it was dominated by the Bruaich, a couple of miles away across the moor. It rose from a broad base by shoulders and buttresses of grey rock, sheer precipices, deep gullies and corries, to a series of ragged peaks three thousand five hundred feet above. Some of the gullies saw the sunlight for an hour or so on a summer's day and never at all in the winter, and snow lay in some of them throughout the year. From the road that ran through the moorland below it could look serene on a gentle summer day. But behind the serenity there was a restlessness, a sense of waiting. On other days, when the strath below was calm, the mist would roll around the peaks, pour down the gullies like a witch's brew and boil silently in the corries. On bad days the corries were filled with the screaming of the wind, and gales savaged the exposed rock faces, and the peaks above were lost in a black swirling darkness. There were days in winter when it could be serene again; an ice palace, crackling with cold, with great snow cornices built by the wind along the ridges. But again there would be a sense of expectancy; a feeling that the mountain was alive, with a personality of its own, dignified and remote, and without mercy.

Over the years since he had taken on the hotel, Cameron had come to regard the Bruaich with a mixture of love and hate: love for its beauty, hatred for what it could do.

There were two men up on the South-east Buttress now. He could see them clearly through the telescope. One of them was wearing a bright red anorak, and they were moving well. He got the impression that they were experienced climbers; and it would be just as well if they were, because they seemed to be heading for the Tower route. They would have a good day for it. There was a moderate wind out of the west, which would affect them little on this side of the Tower, and the fine weather would surely hold up until nightfall, anyhow.

He went back to the telescope two or three times during the day. He saw them a little later on the last pitch going up to the Tower; and again at the base of the Tower, where they would be getting ready to rope down to Agag's Ledge for the traverse. He would have stayed to watch them abseiling; but the telephone went and other things intervened, and when he next looked they were out of sight. They would have made the traverse, he thought, and would be deep in the Tower gully, on their way up to the main peak. He saw no further sign of them until Callum Lithgow came into the hotel in the late afternoon with blood on his clothes and a face like cold porridge and the news that Hamish had come off during the abseil and was lying on the scree below, probably dead.

Sergeant McKechnie followed Sutherland into his room. Sutherland gestured vaguely at a chair and went round to his own chair behind the desk.

'When did it happen?'

'About four o'clock yesterday,' McKechnie said, as he sat down. 'Callum Lithgow came into Iain Cameron's hotel and said his brother had taken a fall on the Bruaich, and he thought he was dead. Iain telephoned us and I sent up Constable Keith. He's our mountaineering expert.'

Sutherland nodded. 'Yes, I know.'

'They got a party together,' McKechnie went on, 'and found Hamish Lithgow at about eight o'clock. He was dead all right.'

'What part of the mountain?'

McKechnie hesitated. He was obviously uncomfortable.

'Go on, man!' Sutherland said irritably. 'I'm not a callow boy.'

'He was on the scree at the foot of the Tower.'

Sutherland said nothing.

McKechnie hesitated again, and then said, 'It seems they were roping down to Agag's Ledge.'

Sutherland remained silent for another moment or two, and then looked up at McKechnie and said briskly, 'No details yet?'

'Not yet. We'll be getting statements. Callum and his wife were badly shaken. They stayed the night at the hotel.'

Sutherland said sharply, 'Was she climbing?'

'No, no. Just the two brothers. Mrs Lithgow happened to be in Glendoran. We got hold of her and she went up with Keith. She was very upset.'

Sutherland sat staring at the papers on his desk. McKechnie watched him for a little and then said quietly, 'You'll not be handling this yourself, Mr Sutherland?'

'I don't think so,' Sutherland said.

'No . . . No need to distress yourself.'

Sutherland looked up suddenly and said, 'Agag's Ledge is a "Very Severe". I didn't know the Lithgows in for that kind of climbing.'

'They climbed a good deal when they were youngsters. Then Hamish was away for some time, you remember. He came back a few months ago when the father died and Callum took over Ruigh.'

'Hamish was the younger brother, wasn't he?'

'No, he was a year older than Callum. But he took no great interest in Ruigh.'

'I see.'

McKechnie rose to his feet. 'I'll pass the report on to Mr Duthie, then. Didn't I hear him say he's done a bit of climbing himself?'

'So I believe,' said Sutherland. 'He might as well make use of it. He can go and take a look at the locus in the meantime.'

'You're a climbing man, Mr Duthie?' Cameron asked.

They were standing at the front of the hotel, looking across the moor at the Bruaich. It was one of the serene days, with only a few wisps of high cirrus cloud in the sky, promising wind later, and the air heavy with the scent of bog-myrtle and warm heather. But to Duthie the sunlight failed to soften the mountain's brooding menace.

'I used to climb quite a bit,' he said.

'A tiger, eh?'

'A tame tiger. I never had enough time.'

'Have you climbed the Bruaich?'

'No.'

Cameron looked at the mountain for a moment. 'It has another name on some of the older maps,' he said. 'In the old Gaelic it was called the Vicious One. It can live up to that, too. Hamish Lithgow wasn't the first. Not by a long chalk. And there will be others.'

'Can you tell me what happened?' Duthie asked.

'Not precisely. Callum wasn't very coherent. He was in great distress. He blamed himself.'

'Why?'

'A piton came out. And it was Callum that put it in. You know what a piton is, of course.'

Duthie knew. A small steel peg with an eyelet at one end, driven into a rock crack and used as an anchorage for the rope. Used with skill it can support the weight of a man, even a man falling. Used carelessly, it can give a man a false sense of security, and betray him.

'Poor devil,' said Duthie, thinking of Callum. 'Can you show me where it happened? Or should I go up and look at it for myself?'

Cameron said, 'I can show you. Come inside.'

They went into the coffee lounge, where he adjusted the telescope. When Duthie looked through it, it framed a massive pinnacle of smooth rock a little below the main peak, with a sheer rock face below it plunging for five or six hundred feet to a steep scree slope.

'You can see the Tower?' Cameron asked.

'Yes.'

'The route is up the steep ridge on the left to the base of the Tower. But you can't climb the Tower from this side except by artificial – pegs and ladders, you know.'

'I know.'

'So you go down on the rope to Agag's Ledge. You'll see it on the cliff face about fifty feet below the Tower.'

Duthie picked out a transverse crack, no more than a hairline in the telescope, crossing the rock wall.

'Yes, I've got it.'

'You traverse to the right until you come to a chimney.'

Duthie found the chimney, a small vertical fissure running slightly obliquely up the cliff face, widening towards its upper end into a deep gully.

'Up the chimney,' said Cameron, 'into the gully at the back of the Tower, and it's an easy scramble from there to the top.'

'What's the traverse like?' Duthie asked.

'Agag's Ledge? Delicate and very exposed. You've got four or five hundred feet of fresh air beneath you.'

'Exactly where did he peel off?'

'Somewhere between the foot of the Tower and Agag's Ledge, while he was roping down.'

'Why rope down? Why not climb?'

'There's a bit of an overhang, for one thing. And the rock below the overhang is very smooth until you get down to the Ledge. There's no more than a few decent holds. Anything else there is would make a fly think twice.'

Duthie tilted the telescope slowly down until it came to the scree at the bottom of the cliff, a steep slope of small, shattered rocks, where Hamish Lithgow had died, probably instantly, in a moment of dreadful impact. He tilted the telescope up again until it framed the rock wall between the foot of the Tower and Agag's Ledge.

'They were roping down,' he said. 'Did they have one of these gadgets, d'you know? A descendeur?'

'I don't know for certain,' Cameron said. 'But I doubt if the Lithgows would have a descendeur. It would be the real thing.'

The real thing, Duthie thought. The classic abseil. You pass the rope through some kind of anchorage – a karabiner clip on a piton or a rope sling round a knob of rock – until it is doubled, so that you can recover it when you get down by pulling it through. You pass the doubled rope between your legs and under your right thigh, obliquely up across your chest and over the left shoulder, obliquely down across the back to your right hand. Then you sit on it and step backwards out into space like a spider on the end of a filament of web. The friction of the rope on your clothing acts as a brake and you go down as fast or as slowly as you like. If you go down too fast you smell burning. If the piton comes out, or if the knob of rock turns out to be rotten, you finish up like Hamish Lithgow. Otherwise, it's foolproof, and fun.

Duthie turned away from the telescope. The coffee lounge was a big room with a wide, open fireplace where the climbers and skiiers would gather round in the winter. There were some good reproductions on the walls and a big photograph of the Bruaich. Duthie went over to it. It had been taken with some kind of telephoto lens and showed the top third of the mountain in remarkable detail. He could trace the route as clearly on it as through the telescope.

'Can I borrow it?' he asked, looking round at Cameron.

'Surely.'

'It might be useful if there's an inquiry.'

'Will there be?'

'I doubt it. It's automatic in some cases, but not, I would say, in this. Although anybody can ask for one. Relatives, for instance. Or the Fiscal can hold one if he thinks there's some safety point that should be aired.'

'I see.' Cameron began to unhitch the photograph from the wall. 'I watched them for a bit through the telescope,' he said.

Duthie looked at him sharply. 'You watched them?'

'I saw them a couple of times. Once when they were going up the ridge. And again a wee while later, when they were getting ready to rope down.'

'You didn't see them actually abseiling?'

'Unfortunately, I was called away. I wouldn't have seen what happened anyhow, even through the telescope.'

'It's a pity, all the same.'

'Yes. I would have been able to give the alarm a bit sooner.'

They went out to the front of the hotel where Duthie's car was parked. Cameron carried the photograph. Duthie stopped on the bridge for a moment and looked at the river. The water ran clear and sparkling over the gravel reaches, into deep pools dark with peat.

'Can I bring a rod sometime and try it?' he asked.

'You can, surely,' said Cameron. 'Plenty of rods here. It's best early in the year, though. But you might still get a trout or two.'

They packed the photograph carefully behind Duthie's seat.

'Take care of it,' Cameron said. 'I took it myself.'

As Duthie was getting into the car he turned suddenly and looked back at the Bruaich. He had the absurd feeling that the mountain had been watching him.

'It's a very good likeness,' Sutherland said.

The photograph was propped up on a chair on the other side of his desk.

'Cameron took it himself,' Duthie said. 'He's caught the light remarkably well.'

'He's had ample opportunity. Staring at it every day of his life.'

'I take it you know the Bruaich.'

'Yes.'

'Who was Agag?'

'You should read your Bible,' Sutherland said. 'He was a gentleman who walked delicately. A desirable accomplishment on the ledge. That's why it's named after him. Have the police got their statements yet?'

'Lithgow's with them now, I believe.'

Sutherland sat for a time, lost in thought. Duthie moved round in front of the photograph and examined it.

'They're a respectable family,' Sutherland said at length.

Duthie straightened up. 'So I understand ... Where is Ruigh?'

'It's about twenty miles up the coast. The Lithgows have farmed it for some generations. I believe the sheep have quite a reputation.'

Duthie said, 'I don't think there's any problem with this. It seems quite straightforward.'

'Good.'

Duthie turned towards the door and Sutherland said sharply, 'Take that damned thing with you!'

Duthie was startled by the suppressed vehemence in Sutherland's voice.

'Sorry,' he said. He came back and picked up the photograph and took it out with him.

Constable Keith was arranging a tidy display of climbing equipment in a corner of the main office as Duthie came out of Sutherland's room. Duthie propped up the photograph on top of a filing cabinet and joined him.

Willie Keith was about twenty-five, a healthy young man with a guileless face. He stood up as Duthie approached.

'That's his gear, Mr Duthie.'

Duthie said, 'Thanks, Willie,' and stood looking at the stuff spread out on the floor.

There was an anorak, dun coloured with patches of faded brown, probably an old Army issue; a pair of boots, nailed with tricounis and muggers, a little heavy by modern standards, but serviceable; a lightweight rucksack; miscellaneous clothing; and a nylon climbing rope of good weight, which looked new. The rope was doubled and neatly coiled. A piton was clipped to it at its mid point by a karabiner, a steel snaplink with a spring gate, used for attaching ropes to a rope sling, a piton, or a climber's waistband.

Keith said, 'The rope's just as we found it. The piton and the karabiner were still on it. He still had a grip on the rope. Instinct, I suppose.'

'What's your opinion?' Duthie asked.

'About what happened?'

'Yes.'

Keith hesitated.

'Off the record,' said Duthie.

'Well, it wouldn't be the first time a piton's come out, would it?'

'What's the rock like on that pitch?'

'It's supposed to be good,' Keith said. 'But you can't always tell, can you?'

'No, I suppose not,' Duthie said. 'Was there a descendeur?'

'I didn't see one. It wasn't on the rope, anyhow.'

'On his waistband?'

'No.'

'So they were doing a classic abseil. They must have had experience.'

'I'm told they had.'

'Okay,' Duthie said. 'Will you ask Sergeant McKechnie to let me have the report as soon as possible?'

'I will, Mr Duthie.'

Keith looked round for his cap, found it and went out.

Duthie went down on one knee and went through the gear carefully, without disturbing Keith's neat arrangement. Then he got to his feet, took out a cigarette, remembered Christine and offered her one. She refused.

'Anything else for me?' Duthie asked.

'It's all on your desk. There's nothing much,' she said. Then she asked, 'Why do people climb? I've never understood it. I mean, this kind of climbing.'

'It's good exercise,' Duthie said.

'You know what I mean,' she said, with a hint of exasperation. 'Anyone who's climbed a bit, this kind of climbing, must know something like this can happen. Why do they keep on doing it?'

'Some people just want to see the view from the top. Or what's on the other side.'

'There must be more to it than that.'

'Well, it is good for you.'

'Being killed?'

'He was unlucky.'

'If he'd been lucky, what would it have meant to him?'

Duthie said, 'Challenge accepted. And an exercise in social relations. When two men go up on to a difficult pitch they have to trust each other completely. One can make a mistake. And the other can die.'

'Is that what happened?'

'Something like that,' said Duthie, and went into his room.

*   *   *

'I blame myself entirely,' Callum Lithgow said.

McKechnie contemplated him for a moment in silence. They were in a small, aseptic room with a scrubbed deal table between them. Two large mugs of tea were on the table. A woman police constable sat quietly in the background with a note-book on her knees. McKechnie knew that the lean, brown man with the alert eyes accustomed to counting sheep was normally contained and taciturn, but was now living on his nerves.

'Do you want that to go into your statement, Mr Lithgow?' he asked. 'I know just how you feel. But put down in black and white, with some stranger reading it, it would sound different.'

Callum gave him a tired smile and said, 'You're not supposed to influence me, are you?'

McKechnie laughed and said, 'Well, we're inside these four walls. And Elsie's a bit hard of hearing.'

The woman police constable smiled faintly, and Callum said, 'Put it down.'

'Are you sure, now?' McKechnie asked.

'Put it down. It's the truth.'

'Very well.' McKechnie waited for a moment or two, then said, 'Is there anything further you would like to add?'

'No. I've told you what happened.'

'Okay.' McKechnie looked round and said, 'Just get that typed up, Elsie, like a good girl.'

She nodded, rose to her feet and went out.

McKechnie got up and began to move around in the confined space, trying to find the words for what he was wanting to say.

'You know this as well as I do, Mr Lithgow. But I'm going to say it all the same. There's no need whatever to go through life with a sense of guilt for something you had no control over.'

Callum watched him in silence.

'Look at it like this,' said McKechnie. 'A bit of rock can look as sound as a bell. But the weather may have been working on it, and who's to know that it's rotten underneath?'

Callum stared at him for a moment. Then his face crumpled and he began to laugh, low and hysterical. McKechnie moved quickly round the table and put a large, comforting hand on his shoulder.

'Pull yourself together, now,' he said. 'And drink your tea.'

Duthie read the police report, and one or two points which he had found a little obscure were clarified when McKechnie was in his office later in the day.

'Callum runs the farm?' Duthie asked.

'That's right. Hamish never took much of an interest in it. He didn't get on too well with his father and he went wandering years ago.'

'Where did he wander?'

'All over the place. Australia, Canada. He came home a few months ago, after the father's death.'

'Has he been working on the farm since then?'

'He wouldn't be straining himself, anyhow. Now and again he'd come into Glendoran when he felt like the bright lights.'

'He liked the bright lights?'

'He was a cheerful man. Good company.'

'And Callum?'

'Like his father,' said McKechnie. 'A nose to the grindstone sort of chap. Shrewd. You won't catch him out. I think it was really Callum that put the Ruigh sheep on the map.'

'He's got a good set-up there?'

'It's a good set-up, all right. And he's worked like a beaver for it.'

'Happily married?'

'I would say so. She's a bright kind of girl.'

'Children?'

'Not yet.'

'And relations between the brothers were good?'

McKechnie pondered for a moment. 'I never heard anything to the contrary. I would say they were. They were close as youngsters. Went climbing a lot together, for example. But you never could really tell with Callum. He's all wrapped up in Ruigh. I doubt if he's got any real regard now for anything outside of it.'

Duthie thought for a little. 'Well, that seems to have cleared everything up,' he said.

'Will you be wanting to talk to him yourself?'

'I don't think so. If I do, we can get him.'

'No difficulty, Mr Duthie. Just let me know.'

Duthie thanked him and McKechnie went out. Duthie began to read through the report again before taking it in to Sutherland.

McKechnie stopped on his way through the main office and looked at Keith's display of equipment. It was all good gear, he thought, the kind of thing you would expect with experienced climbers. He said so to Christine.

'I wouldn't know,' she said. 'I never climb anything higher than a ladder. And only if it's in a good cause. Like Christmas.'

McKechnie laughed. 'You'd be surprised, though, the way some people go up into the hills after all the warnings and publicity. In clothes that wouldn't keep out a shower at a manse garden party. In gym shoes. So that they turn an ankle and half a dozen men have to give up the best part of a working day to go up and carry them down. It's not just thoughtlessness. It's damned stupidity.'

He squatted down on his heels as he spoke, and was examining the rope. Doubled, as it had been for the abseil, and coiled neatly by Keith, the two ends now lay close together. McKechnie picked them up and studied them. One end had been neatly whipped with strong twine. The other had been sealed with heat, a candle flame or a match, so that the fibres had melted and congealed together. Nylon was often enough finished off in this way – by climbers or by amateur yachtsmen – when there was too little time or inclination to make a tidy job of it. But somebody had taken plenty of time with the other end. Why? McKechnie sat on his heels and thought about it until he heard Sutherland's voice behind him.

'You've spotted it too?'

McKechnie laid down the rope and rose to his feet as Sutherland crossed from the door of his room.

'I was wondering about it,' he said.

'It probably has no significance at all. But it's one of those infuriating things. Once you've noticed it, it keeps intruding.'

'I was thinking,' said McKechnie, 'that Callum might have done one end and Hamish the other.'

'Sound logic. It's in character. Has Mr Duthie got the report yet?'

'I just gave it to him.'

'Good. I'll go over it with him.' As he turned back to his room he said to Christine, 'You might ask him to come in when he's ready.'

Duthie came in with the report ten minutes later.

'D'you want to read it?' he asked.

'No. You tell me. Just the bones.'

Duthie opened the file containing the report.

'The usual thing about finding the body and so on. Constable Keith took a party up from the Lairig Hotel to the scree slope at the foot of the Tower Wall, where they found Hamish Lithgow dead. There's a point about the rope.'

'Yes?'

'The piton and the karabiner were still on it.'

Sutherland looked at Duthie hopefully for a moment.

'Nothing else?'

'No.'

'Have you examined the rope?' Sutherland asked.

'Briefly.'

'Take another look at it. It could be a nice example of fraternal cooperation. Go on.'

Duthie referred to the file, then went on. 'Callum Lithgow was deeply distressed when making his statement. He blames himself for what happened.'

'The distress is a normal reaction, surely. Any particular reason for blaming himself?'

'He was leading. And he put in the piton. Also, he feels responsible because Hamish was out of practice. This was his first climb since he came back to Ruigh after some years absence.'

'Whose idea was this expedition?'

'Hamish's. Mrs Lithgow confirms that.'

'The Bruaich's a tough starter.'

'They'd climbed there before,' Duthie said. 'They knew the route.'

'It's no route for a man out of practice.'

'Apparently there's only one bad pitch on it.'

'If you include the abseil and the Ledge as one. And that's a very bad pitch. You've seen it, haven't you?'

'From the hotel.'

'You didn't go up to it?'

'I didn't think it necessary.'

'It might be worth it.'

'Still . . . Well, you may be right. What does Callum say, then?'

'He put in the piton. Roped down to Agag's Ledge. Then to give his brother room on the Ledge he began the traverse.'

'With no safety rope?'

'Hamish was using it to rope down. Anyhow, I gather the first bit of the traverse is easy.'

'That's right.'

Duthie looked at him curiously. It had just occurred to him that Sutherland seemed to know what he was talking about.

'You know this route pretty well,' he said.

'Intimately,' said Sutherland. 'Go on.'

Duthie looked at the file again.

'Hamish was about half way down when the piton came out. He went straight past Callum to the scree at the foot. Callum got there as fast as he could. But there was nothing he could do. So he went down to the hotel, and Iain Cameron called the Glendoran police.'

Sutherland tilted his chair back and balanced it carefully on two legs. He was staring at the far wall, with a blank look in his eyes. Duthie watched him in silence. He had the impression that Sutherland had lost interest and had allowed his mind to wander away to something quite remote in time and place; until Sutherland said in a curiously flat voice:

'When an experienced man goes climbing on a mountain like the Bruaich he accepts the element of danger. It's part of the deal.'

'That's what I think,' Duthie said. For some reason, he found the remark unexpected.

'Sometimes it can be a damned rough deal,' Sutherland said. 'Without reason or logic or justice. You can't foresee it. You can't fight it. You can only wonder till the end of your days at the malevolence of an inanimate object like a mountain.' He let his chair tilt forward again with a small thud and said briskly, 'It's up to you. An inquiry?'

After a moment Duthie said, 'I think it would be a waste of public money.'

'I'm inclined to agree. Either Hamish Lithgow checked the piton before he started to rope down. Or he didn't. If he didn't, it was his own fault.'

'Right.'

'All the same, there's something I'd like you to look at,' Sutherland said, and got to his feet.

Duthie followed him out of the room and across the main office to the corner where Hamish Lithgow's climbing gear lay. Sutherland picked up the two ends of the rope and held them, one in either hand, for Duthie to see.

'One end seamanlike,' he said. 'The other a dog's breakfast.'

'Yes, I see that,' Duthie said. He grinned faintly and added, 'Now.'

Sutherland said, 'This end sealed by heat. One of the advantages of nylon rope. A couple of matches would do it. If you're lucky it doesn't stick to your fingers and take the skin off. A farmer's job, would you say?'

'Could be,' said Duthie, cautiously.

'This other end has been neatly whipped. And not common whipping, mark you. Palm and needle work. A sailor's job. No landlubber did this.'

'Hamish, presumably. It's reasonable. One of them did one end. The other one did the other.'

'Yes. I suppose that's the obvious conclusion.'

'Why d'you think it's interesting?'

'I don't know,' said Sutherland. 'It just is.'

He began to pass the rope through his hands, examining it, letting it drop again in neat coils, still doubled.

'New rope,' he said. 'In excellent condition. They weren't taking any chances with this, anyhow.'

When he came to the end, where the karabiner and piton were still on the rope, he inspected them briefly, then laid them down. He stood looking down at the rope for a moment, then looked round at Duthie. He was frowning very slightly, as though something at the back of his mind troubled him.

'You say Callum roped directly to Agag's Ledge?'

'Yes.'

'Is there a court tomorrow?'

'Tomorrow? No.'

'Then I think it might be worth having him in for a chat. Say ten o'clock?'

Duthie looked across the room at Christine. She picked up the telephone.

VIII

'Sugar, Mr Lithgow?' Duthie asked.

'Not for me thanks.'

Callum Lithgow was sitting in one of the comfortable chairs beside Sutherland's desk, balancing a mug on his knee. Duthie offered the sugar bowl to Sutherland, who took one spoonful and stirred it slowly. Duthie took three and said, 'I finally gave up sugar several years ago. I've been giving it up at frequent intervals ever since.'

It was not a very witty remark, but it was an icebreaker and Callum laughed as though glad of the opportunity.

Sutherland sat drinking tea and watching him.

'Your brother was an experienced climber,' he said presently.

'Yes, when he was younger.'

'Did you climb together a great deal?'

'Yes. Up till the time he left. He'd be coming on for about twenty then.'

'Were you very close?'

Callum smiled slightly. 'Yes and no. We were brothers. But we were different. Hamish got on well with people.'

'Don't you?'

'Well enough. I don't have much time for the social life. Ruigh keeps me pretty well occupied.' He added in a low voice, 'But I got on well with Hamish.'

'Was he on good terms with your wife?'

'Oh, yes. Indeed, we would have liked it fine if he would have stayed on at Ruigh. But he had a kind of a notion to go back to Canada sometime. He was beginning to do well there.'

'Were you satisfied that he was in good enough condition to attempt a difficult climb like the Tower route on the Bruaich?'

Callum hesitated. 'Well, no, not really. He was in good condition physically. But he was out of practice. He'd done no climbing since he went away. But he was dead keen to try it. So I thought if I would lead and kind of keep an eye on him it would be all right.' He made a small helpless gesture with his hands and said, 'I wish to God I had said no to it!'

Sutherland said, 'I don't think you should blame yourself too much for that. After all, he was no beginner. He knew what he was up against.'

'Yes, he knew that all right. We'd done the Tower before.'

'It was you who put in the piton,' Sutherland said.

Callum nodded. 'Yes.' He was silent for a moment. Then he went on, 'I thought it was in right, Mr Sutherland. I thought it was sound. It sang as it went in. You can tell.'

'I'm told the singing note of a piton going in isn't always a reliable guide.'

'That's quite true. But it doesn't sing if it's not going in right. That's the point.'

'I suppose you tested it carefully before you roped down?'

Callum said dryly, 'That wall goes straight down for four or five hundred feet.'

'So you tested it and then roped down to Agag's Ledge?'

'Yes.'

'Did you have any difficulty when you roped down?'

Callum frowned. 'Difficulty?'

Sutherland said, 'You had no problem of any kind that might have put additional strain on the piton? Weakened it a little? Dislodged it slightly?'

Callum thought for a moment. 'No, there was no problem. Except that it's not an easy abseil. There's a bit of an overhang. And you're roping down to a ledge that's not exactly like a railway station platform.'

'I appreciate that,' said Sutherland. 'You must forgive me if I seem a little fussy. I just want to get a clear picture in my head. You roped directly down to Agag's Ledge. Then you traversed along it a little way in order to give your brother room. Am I right?'

'Quite right.'

'Did your brother check the piton before he started to abseil?'

'Yes.'

'How d'you know? You were about fifty feet below him, on the Ledge. And as you say, there's a bit of an overhang. You couldn't see him.'

Callum said quietly, 'He was a careful climber, Mr Sutherland. I knew him.'

'But the piton came out. And he fell.'

Callum nodded. 'I know what you're saying, Mr Sutherland. And you're right. It was my fault. He could have got out of the habit. I should have made him go down first. I would have double checked that piton. It was me that was careless. And I'll never forgive myself.'

'Possibly not, Mr Lithgow,' Sutherland said quietly. 'Possibly not. These things tend to stay with us for ever.'

Callum gave him a sudden, curious look.

'But when men climb mountains,' Sutherland said, 'they must accept that there may be totally unexpected hazards. Don't you agree?'

Callum was silent. Duthie, slightly puzzled, looked at Sutherland, and then at Callum. He had the odd feeling that he had suddenly been excluded.

Sutherland rose to his feet. 'Anyhow, we've kept you long enough. It's been a distressing experience for you. I don't suppose you enjoy talking about it. I'm sure you'll be glad to get home to Ruigh.'

As Callum got up Duthie took his empty tea mug and put it on the tray. Sutherland moved round the desk towards the door.

'How's Mrs Lithgow bearing up?' he asked.

'She's taking it very hard. It was good for her to have some-one like Hamish around. It's all work at Ruigh, you know. And she liked him.'

'I'm sure she did. Like everybody else, from what I hear.'

Callum hesitated in the doorway. 'Will there be an inquiry or anything? I mean, can I make arrangements . . . for Hamish?'

Sutherland said carefully, 'I think you should proceed on the assumption that there won't be any difficulty.'

'Thank you, Mr Sutherland.'

Sutherland nodded and said, 'See Mr Lithgow out, Alec.'

Duthie went out with Callum. Sutherland closed the door behind them and returned to his desk. He shuffled through the papers on it a little aimlessly for a moment or two, in an effort to get back to the routine of work. But he knew it to be futile, and gave up. He opened a drawer and took out a leather folder. It contained, on one side, a photograph of himself, taken about five years ago; and on the other side, the photograph of a handsome woman, two or three years younger. He set it up on the desk and sat back, debating whether to leave it there, or to keep it hidden. As he had kept it for years.

McKechnie and Constable Keith had been waiting for some time. Christine took pity on them, recovered the tea tray from Sutherland's room and made tea. She set it down for them on a small table.

'I told Mr Duthie this place was just a glorified tea bar,' she said. 'It's been worse since he came.'

'You get through a good deal of other work on the side,' McKechnie said comfortingly.

Christine smiled and returned to her typewriter. McKechnie handed a mug to Keith.

Keith said, 'D'you think Mr Sutherland's going to take

over this Bruaich business, then? I mean, with him interviewing Callum Lithgow, it looks a bit like it.'

'I hope not,' said McKechnie.

Christine looked at him briefly.

'Why?' Keith asked.

McKechnie took his time before he said, 'How long is it since you came to Glendoran?'

'Three years,' said Keith.

McKechnie nodded and began to drink his tea. Keith waited for a moment and then began to shovel sugar into his tea mug.

McKechnie said, 'You'll put on weight, son. Then you won't be able to climb mountains.'

Keith grinned. 'You're wrong, sarge. It gives you energy.'

Duthie came in through the outside door. Christine looked up from her typewriter.

'Is he all right?' she asked.

'He took a bit of calming down. I think he felt the Fiscal was a bit rough with him.'

'Was he?'

Duthie shrugged. 'I don't know. He's got some kind of bee in his bonnet.' He looked round at McKechnie and said, 'I'm sorry. You've been waiting.'

'That's all right, Mr Duthie. There's just one or two things I'd like to get cleared up. There's the question of bail for James Brown. His good lady's at the station now, foaming at the mouth.'

Duthie said, 'Give me a minute to get some tea,' and went into the filing cupboard.

In his own room, Sutherland came to a decision and got to his feet. For the past twenty-four hours there had been a maggot in his mind. It had been troubling him increasingly, and he decided it was time to get rid of it. He came into the main office as Duthie came out of the filing cupboard with a mug in his hand.

'How long is that rope?' Sutherland asked. 'The abseil rope?'

Duthie was taken by surprise. 'I don't know. I didn't measure it.' He looked round at McKechnie. 'I expect the police did.'

McKechnie looked at Keith.

Keith said, 'Yes, sir. Eighty-one feet. The usual length's a hundred and twenty upwards. But there's no really long pitches on the route they were on . . .'

'They had to rope down to Agag's Ledge,' Sutherland said. 'With the rope doubled. That gives them forty feet, six inches. He's lying, Duthie. He couldn't do it.'

Keith said, 'Well, it might be a bit tight, but . . .'

'Have you ever climbed that route?' Sutherland asked.

'No, not exactly that route, sir . . .'

'Then don't talk nonsense.'

'He could have free-climbed the last few feet,' Duthie suggested.

'I made a point of it,' Sutherland said. 'He said he roped directly down to the Ledge without problems. Anyone climbing the rock above Agag's Ledge has problems.'

Duthie frowned and laid his tea mug on a corner of Christine's desk.

'Why should he lie?' he asked reasonably.

'Why does anybody lie?'

'He was willing enough to take the blame.'

Sutherland snorted. 'For a piton coming out? That's nothing.'

'It did come out,' Duthie said, still reasonably.

'Of course it came out. Pitons do come out. They're generally taken out where possible after they've served their purpose, because they cost money and can be used again. And a good thing, too. Otherwise Scotland, the Alps, the Dolomites and the Himalayas would be nothing but picturesque pincushions by now. But I suggest this one was taken out to conceal the truth.'

'What truth?' Duthie asked.

'I don't know. But suppose Callum let his brother go down first. And suppose Hamish ran out of abseil rope.'

Duthie looked shocked. 'That's pure speculation.'

Sutherland gave him a cold stare. 'You think so? Well, accept it for the moment. Would that not be culpable? Would that not be something to conceal?'

Duthie said, 'Would it?'

'Callum knew the route better,' Sutherland said. 'Hamish hadn't climbed it for some years. It seemed to me that Callum knew it very well. And he must have known that forty feet of rope wasn't enough.'

'But there's no evidence at all that Callum wasn't leading. That he didn't abseil first. As he claims.'

'There's no evidence to the contrary. It's not unusual for the second man to pass through and lead for a time, to rest the leader. As far as evidence goes, that could have happened. Hamish could have gone down first.'

'And run out of rope? Suppose that happened. You could call it culpable. But it could have been a lapse of memory. It could have been a simple misjudgement.'

'Then why conceal it?'

'Human frailty. He might even be trying to conceal it from himself.'

'He didn't try to conceal that he was responsible for putting in the piton.'

'What are you trying to do to him?' Duthie asked, with an edge of exasperation in his voice. 'I thought you said justice without compassion is a fraud.'

'There is a possible alternative,' Sutherland said. 'But it's uglier.'

He picked up Duthie's tea mug, drank and made a wry face. 'You've put too much sugar in,' he said to Christine.

She was about to protest but decided not to.

'I'm sorry,' she said. 'I'll get you another.'

'I've often thought,' Sutherland said, 'that the ideal way to commit murder is to take your intended up on to a mountain and push him over a steep place. No witnesses. Except you and God.' He looked at Duthie. 'And I have no compassion for murder.'

'Good God!' Duthie said. 'You don't knock off your brother just because he doesn't like your sheep. There isn't a shred of hard evidence that Callum's lying. What is this bee you've got in your bonnet? You always bawl me out when I speculate . . .'

'I'm not speculating,' Sutherland said quietly. 'He quite

deliberately lied. He could not have abseiled down to Agag's Ledge on that length of rope.'

Duthie shrugged and said, 'You'll never prove it, anyhow. One way or the other.'

'We can try,' said Sutherland. 'Indeed, we have a duty to.'

Duthie had a sudden feeling of uneasiness.

'How?' he asked.

'We can inspect the locus. We can follow their route step by step.' He gave Duthie a long, somewhat calculating look, and added, 'Using Callum's rope.'

Duthie was silent, digesting this. After a moment, McKechnie said uncomfortably, 'You, sir?'

'Yes.'

'I'm sure Constable Keith would be glad to take Mr Duthie up the Bruaich if you don't feel like it, sir.'

Sutherland smiled at him. 'I'm sure he would. But I do feel like it. It's high time I squared things with that lump of schist and porphyry.'

Christine was standing in the doorway of the filing cupboard with a mug of tea in her hand, staring at him.

'I'll take it in my room, if you don't mind,' Sutherland said to her, and turned and went inside.

The brass telescope swept slowly over the face of the Bruaich. It was a bright, brittle day, with every crack and chimney in the great rock walls picked out in sharp relief. But it was like the days of one's youth, Cameron thought: deceptive. The breeze was out of the west, with a moan in it. Later, the corries would be dark and filled with the echoing sound of falling water. Later still, black nimbus clouds would build up in the west and the wind would gust, bending the rowan trees by the river and driving sheets of rain before it. But that would not be until the evening.

The telescope stopped as it discovered two small figures plodding up the lower slopes of the South-east Buttress. Cameron watched them for a bit. They seemed to be making for the Tower route. He wondered, as he often did, at the determination of people who climbed mountains. It was not ten days since a man had died below the Tower, and here were others on the same ploy. They would have a good enough day for it. They were away to an early start and should be off the mountain by late afternoon. If they were any longer, it would be rough going.

As he straightened up he saw a car on the winding road that led in from the main road to the hotel and turned the telescope on it. It was a police car, so he decided to go out and meet it. He tapped the barometer on the way to the door, and didn't like its message.

He waited by the bridge over the river. It was the sort of day when sound carried. He could hear the small burns on the hillside behind, and a cock grouse barking away out in the heather, and cars on the main road almost a mile away. The police car appeared suddenly out of a dip in the side road, crossed the bridge and stopped. Constable Keith got out.

'Hello, Willie,' said Cameron. '*Cia mar a tha u?*'

'*Tha gu math*, Mr Cameron,' said Keith, and grinned. He had been studying the Gaelic for some months, but it was still strange on his tongue.

'I see there's a couple of climbers on the Bruaich,' said Cameron.

'It's the Fiscal and Mr Duthie.'

Cameron looked at him sharply and Keith saw the astonishment in his eyes.

'I've to come and pick them up here at six,' he said. 'They're going up to take a look at where it happened.'

Cameron said nothing. He turned and looked at the mountain.

'I didn't know Mr Sutherland was a climber,' Keith said.

'He was,' said Cameron slowly. 'A very good one. There's more than one route up north in his own part of the country with his name on it.'

After a moment Keith said, 'Sergeant McKechnie didn't seem to like the idea of him going up the Bruaich, though.'

'Neither do I,' said Cameron.

'He told me to look in and tell you that I would be on duty all day, if you need me.'

Cameron nodded. He was looking through half-closed eyes, trying to pick out the small figures on the South-east Buttress. But it was too far. The mountain was pale grey in this light, and looked peaceful.

Angus McInnes was looking at the Bruaich too. But he was looking at the other side of it and from some miles away across the firth. McKechnie and Constable Ross had come over on the early boat and the three of them were now on the spread of gravel in front of the house. McKechnie was carrying a small suitcase containing a few of Angus's personal things. Ross was making a lead for the collie with a piece of string.

'Tell him we'll take good care of the dog,' McKechnie said. Then he had a thought and added, 'Indeed, you can tell him it will be a guest in my own house for as long as necessary.'

Ross translated. Angus nodded, gave McKechnie a quick look and turned back to the view. He surveyed it slowly, the firth and the islands and the distant mountains backed by the Bruaich, as though he might be seeing it for the last time. He was, after all, eighty years old and had no idea at all of what the coming months held for him.

Ross had completed the lead for the dog and was ready. McKechnie waited for a few moments longer. Then he turned and checked the door to make sure it was locked, turned back to Angus and said, 'Okay?' Angus nodded and they began to walk down the track. Ross followed, leading the dog.

Duthie had assumed that he would have to match his pace to Sutherland's. Ease off a little now and again, without making it obvious, to let the Old Man keep up. He discovered with some irritation that in spite of the twenty years between them Sutherland's long hill stride, with the feet planted solidly, heel and toe touching ground at the same time, was stretching him to his limit.

They were on the steep slog up the buttress, following a track made by generations of climbers, which wound up through the heather and small broken rock, dodging minor outcrops and escarpments, as though to conserve energy for the high crags above. They could see nothing of the Bruaich peaks from here; they were hidden behind the mass of the buttress, but Duthie was aware of a big corrie over to the right, mainly by sound, the muted sound of a cascade, the occasional echoing rattle of a falling rock. The country behind and below had opened out into a great sweep of brown and purple moor, speckled with the silver of lochans and small rivers, walled in by other mountain ranges. Over the ridge behind the Lairig Hotel the peaks stretched away to the north, to the great hump of Ben Nevis.

Presently they came over the shoulder at the top of the buttress and the ground levelled out on to a small plateau. The great rock pinnacles of the summit loomed above them. The smooth face of the Tower was about half a mile away at the end of a narrow, curved ridge, which was really the lip of the corrie. To the right the ridge dropped sheer to the floor of the corrie. To the left it fell away in a series of steep slabs to a green valley and the head of one of the fjord-like sea lochs that indent the coast.

They walked to the lip of the corrie. The depths were gloomy and oppressive, even on a bright day. Duthie could see the scree slope at the foot of the Tower wall, where Hamish had died. He was a little shaken. It seemed incredibly far below, for a Scottish mountain. He had seen this sort of thing in the Dolomites, where he had spent a month during his university days. But never before in this country.

He made a remark about it, but Sutherland was staring into the corrie and did not seem to hear. There was an intensity in his face which, for some reason, stopped Duthie from repeating it.

He was feeling the exhilaration which always came to him on a mountain, a sense of freedom and space and distance. He could see the Lairig Hotel beyond the corrie, across the moors, a small cluster of white buildings. Nearer, toy cars were crawling on the main road. Above and to the south and east the sky was a bright, clear blue. To the west it was veiled and pearl grey. He decided that this was a heat haze. But he was wrong.

They heard a voice shouting in the distance, from somewhere below, echoing and re-echoing among the cliffs. They searched and saw two small figures in brightly coloured anoraks far down in the corrie on the opposite side. One of them was waving. They waved back, and heard the voice again, shouting something.

'I can't make it out,' Duthie said.

'Climbers going off the mountain,' said Sutherland. 'They don't trust the weather. D'you want to turn back?'

Duthie was surprised. 'No. It looks all right to me.'

'We'll press on, then. I think we'll just have time.'

The two anoraks down in the corrie had begun to move again, down towards the lower slopes.

Sutherland began to move out on to the ridge.

'Watch it here,' he said. 'It gets very exposed once you get out a bit.'

Duthie followed him. He had never suffered from vertigo, but he kept a respectable yard or two between himself and the plunging emptiness on his right.

Cameron had watched them from time to time during the morning. He had watched the glass, too, dropping slowly, and the pearl grey sky beyond the shoulders of the Bruaich darkening as the day went on. He had watched the alders and the rowans by the river bending in a stiffening breeze, and the bog cotton, the white canna, the canna bawn of the ancients, dancing in the peat hags. He was uneasy, though he knew that Sutherland's knowledge of the Bruaich and its moods was as good as his own. But it had beaten him once, and might beat him again.

At noon he had seen them come up on to the shoulder above the South-east Buttress, and a little later he had watched them on the ridge approaching the Tower. And now he could see them at the base of the Tower, above Agag's Ledge; and he was tempted to call Willie Keith, who would be on duty at Glendoran and waiting for it. Not because he thought the weather was going to close in on them yet, or because he could see any sign that they were in difficulty; but just because he was ill at ease about the whole business.

*

'You see why it needs pegs and ladders,' Sutherland said.

'Yes,' said Duthie.

The ridge had brought them to a ledge four or five feet wide between the bottom of the Tower and the sheer drop into the corrie. The face of the Tower above them seemed to Duthie to overhang slightly. There were one or two fissures and cracks in the lower part which he felt might be climbable, but he was prepared to accept that they might lead on to a wall that could be attacked only by artificial means.

'So we have to rope down to Agag's Ledge,' Sutherland said. 'It's fifty feet, give or take a foot. The traverse along the Ledge is delicate and exposed, but reasonable. It leads to a fairly easy chimney. You can see the upper part of it along there.'

Duthie saw it, forty or fifty yards away, rising obliquely and disappearing out of sight somewhere behind the Tower. He moved cautiously to the edge of the shelf on which they were standing and looked down. The Ledge itself was hidden by overhanging rock immediately below the shelf; but a long way down he could see the scree and some of the lower part of the rock wall above it.

'I give you my word,' Sutherland said. 'It's there all right.'

Duthie grinned and turned. Sutherland was searching the rock behind them for some indication of where Callum's piton might have been inserted; but there had been too many used here over the years, one or two of which were still in place. So he gave up and looked for a suitable crack which they could now use for themselves. When he had found one that pleased him, he took one of the pitons from the line slung round his shoulder and began to drive it in with a light piton hammer. It went in with a clear, singing note on each stroke. The sound echoed back from the walls of the corrie.

They both had a coil of climbing rope on their shoulders. Duthie began to unship his.

'We use Callum's rope,' he said.

Sutherland gave a final blow to the piton and said, 'I'm not sure if it would be wise.'

'Why not?'

'Call it second thoughts, if you like.'

'But that's why we brought it,' Duthie said, a little impatiently.

'I know that. But I just don't fancy running out of rope two-thirds of the way down.'

Duthie said, 'You don't need to. I'll take a chance. You still haven't convinced me.'

'If anybody goes down on Callum's rope,' Sutherland said, 'I'll go. I've done this route before.'

He selected a karabiner and clipped it into the piton.

'I'm a little younger,' Duthie said.

'I have that in mind too,' Sutherland said. 'I hate to see youth cut off in its flower.'

'How long is it since you climbed here?'

'Five years.'

'You're out of training. I've climbed a good deal since then.'

Sutherland said nothing. He was examining Callum's rope, which now lay in a neat coil on the shelf. He picked up the burnt end and began to thread it through the karabiner.

'You've marked the mid point?' he asked.

'Yes.'

Sutherland led about seven feet of rope through the karabiner. Then he gripped the doubled rope firmly just below the karabiner and slid his hand down until it came to the burnt end. He pulled the doubled rope taut and held it out. The burnt end reached exactly to the edge of the shelf.

'Put the rest over the side,' he said.

Duthie hesitated.

'Go on,' Sutherland said sharply. 'Just do it.'

He held the doubled rope firmly. Duthie let the rest of the rope carefully over the edge. It snaked down out of sight.

'How much is below now?' Sutherland asked.

Duthie eyed the doubled rope between the karabiner and the edge, estimating it.

Sutherland sat on his heels, holding the rope taut.

'You've got about seven feet between the piton and the edge,' Duthie said. 'Doubled, that makes fourteen feet. So there's between sixty and seventy feet below.'

'Thank you,' said Sutherland, and straightened up. 'Enough

to take you comfortably down to Agag's Ledge,' he said. 'Without problems. So there's sixty odd feet missing from here.' And he indicated the burnt end.

Duthie said, 'Missing?'

'He cut it. Probably with a piton hammer against a sharp edge. Like that one.'

He pointed with a foot at a small knife-edge of rock. He began to lead more rope through the karabiner.

Duthie was silent for a moment. The wind had freshened considerably since they had crossed the ridge, tugging at their clothing and gusting down in the corrie with a low moaning sound.

Duthie said, 'You're making it all too easy. You're making it fit your own theories.'

'It does fit. You'll accept that, surely.'

'No, I don't! We don't even know for certain the rope's too short. We've only your recollection for it. And you say it's five years. Your memory. Unsupported. It's not enough.'

'I've a very clear memory,' Sutherland said.

'Is this my case?' Duthie asked.

'Unless you want to back out.'

'I don't. But it's not murder as far as I'm concerned until I get some real evidence.'

Sutherland contemplated him for a moment, with something like sympathy in his eyes.

'All right,' he said. 'Go and get it.'

He had passed the rope through the karabiner until he had come to the scrap of coloured cloth marking the mid point. He tossed the rest of the rope over the side, so that it hung doubled, ready for the abseil.

A spatter of heavy raindrops hit the picture window. Cameron straightened up from the telescope and made up his mind.

There was a small cocktail bar in one corner of the room, with a telephone on one of the shelves at the back. Cameron went over to it and started to make a call.

About ten minutes later Willie Keith came into the main office where Christine was typing.

'I'm just going up to the Lairig Hotel,' he said. 'Like to come along for the ride?'

Christine looked at her watch. 'You're early, aren't you?' she said.

'Iain Cameron phoned. He thought they might be coming off the Bruaich a bit sooner than they expected.'

There was tension in her voice as she asked, 'There's nothing wrong, is there?'

'No, no. It's just that the weather's getting a bit dicey.'

Christine got to her feet.

'Finish what you're doing,' Keith said. 'There's no great hurry.'

'Isn't there?'

Keith grinned. 'There's nothing to worry about. They'll just get a bit wet.'

She looked at him curiously. 'Don't you know what happened the last time he was on that mountain?' she asked.

Sutherland had made a spike belay with the main climbing rope. One end was attached to his waistband, and from there passed round a solid knob of rock with a figure-of-eight knot, thus securing Sutherland. The other end of the rope would be attached to Duthie's waistband; Sutherland would pay it out as Duthie went down, passing the rope over one shoulder and across his back, so that he could brake it by friction if Duthie came off.

Sutherland was checking his knots. He was being meticulous. Duthie thought, overdoing it a little. He picked up the end of the safety-rope and was about to attach it to his waistband when Sutherland stopped him.

'I'll do that,' Sutherland said sharply.

Duthie said, irritably, 'Damn it, I can tie a knot.'

'I'm sure you can. But you're not going to tie this one.'

He began to tie the safety-rope to Duthie's waistband with a Tarbuck knot. Duthie felt anger rising in him. He had a curious feeling that what Sutherland was trying to prove had nothing whatever to do with Callum or Hamish Lithgow.

'What is the matter with you?' he said.

134

Sutherland completed the knot without replying. He checked it carefully. Then he adjusted the safety-rope around himself in a shoulder belay.

'All right,' he said.

A damp gust of wind came up from the corrie below and a flurry of rain hit them.

'Want to give up?' Sutherland asked.

'No,' Duthie said.

He began to adjust the doubled rope from the piton around himself in the classic abseil position.

Sutherland said, 'There are other ways of doing it.'

'Wait for better weather?' said Duthie. 'Or get Constable Keith? You turned him down. Remember?'

'Yes, I know.'

Duthie stared at him with a sense of futility and mounting antagonism. What in God's name was he doing, he wondered, standing here on a ridiculous shelf of rock with five hundred feet of sweet damn all beneath him, on a day that had suddenly turned lousy, merely because Sutherland had developed some theory based on bits and pieces of circumstantial evidence, which was probably wrong.

'What are you trying to prove, anyhow?' he said. 'It's not just Callum. It's something else.'

'I'm not trying to prove anything. I just want to know what happened.'

'For God's sake, I know what happened! Callum told us. It makes sense. Why don't you believe him?'

'Because he's lying, Duthie. Go on. Find out for yourself.'

Duthie still hesitated, not because he was afraid, although he was; but because for some absurd reason he wanted to continue the argument and find out what it was really all about.

'There may come a point when it will comfort you to know that you're securely belayed this time,' Sutherland said.

Duthie said sharply, 'This time?'

Sutherland stared at him, and said, 'Go on, damn you!'

Duthie took a firm grip on the doubled rope, Callum's rope, and walked backwards over the edge.

*

Keith was at the brass telescope, but he could see very little. The Bruaich was dark and remote, although it was only three in the afternoon, and cloud vapour was boiling sluggishly down through the high gullies into the corrie. He straightened up. Christine was standing at the window. She looked round at him, and Keith shrugged.

Cameron came across the room from the bar in the corner. He had a tray with two glasses on it.

'This'll warm you up, Miss Russell,' he said.

Christine thanked him and took one of the glasses.

'A wee dram for you, Willie,' said Cameron.

Keith took the other glass and said, 'There's no sign of them. The visibility's right down.'

'The last time I caught sight of them,' Cameron said, 'they were just getting ready to come down to Agag's Ledge.'

Christine looked at him doubtfully. 'You don't think anything's gone wrong?'

'No, I don't think so at all. The Fiscal's a real good climber. And I'm sure Mr Duthie knows what he's doing.'

'I hope so,' she said, and turned to look out of the window again at the dark, sullen mass of the mountain.

Duthie found himself hanging in space below the overhang, several feet out from the rock wall. He had expected it, but he was shocked by the sudden, dreadful loneliness. The corrie had grown very dark. Fingers of cloud were creeping down from above, spilling out of the gullies. He was enveloped in sound, which he hadn't noticed before. The loud sound of falling water, tossed back from the cliffs around him. Strange muffled sounds came up from the corrie floor. Falling rocks, he thought, but if they kept falling at this rate there wouldn't be any damned mountain left.

He let himself down slowly, feeling the harsh rub of the rope across his back and under his thigh. I'll burst into flames, he thought, and laughed, and at the same moment his feet touched the rock wall. It was smooth, without footholds, damp and sweating like the palms of his hands, but it was astonishingly comforting, and he began to enjoy himself. He walked slowly down the wall, half backwards, half sideways, looking down. He could see Agag's Ledge now, twenty or thirty feet below. It was about a foot wide at the point where he would reach it. Below it, the wall dropped at what seemed to be a slightly easier gradient down to the scree on the corrie floor. And then he became aware that he was about to run out of abseil rope.

Sutherland was tense and absorbed as he paid out the safety-rope. He was hardly conscious of the lash of the wind and of the rain which was now driving steadily. By the feel of the rope, and from his memory of the pitch below, he was aware almost foot by foot of what Duthie was doing. And he knew, almost as soon as Duthie did, that he had come to the end of the abseil rope. He felt a small surge of satisfaction, touched with guilt for having exposed Duthie to what might now be an extremely uncomfortable fifteen minutes. He did not rate it higher than that. Duthie was on the end of a good safety-rope, well belayed. Whatever happened, he could be got down to Agag's Ledge, and the wall below that could be climbed, given time and care. He waited, tense and prepared, because he felt it was at least possible that Duthie would come off.

Duthie waited too. He was still on the abseil rope; but within a few moments he would have to abandon it. He examined the rock wall above, and the overhang, and realized that he was on a non-reversible route. Except by the tedious business of prusiking up the abseil rope, which he had no intention of attempting, if only to deny Sutherland the pleasure of laughing at him when he got to the top again. He examined the wall below and saw that there were a few holds, not many, not good, and badly spaced. But he decided he could make it. So he abandoned Callum Lithgow's rope and climbed with an intensity of concentration that he had never had to use before; hardly aware of the wind now driving viciously across the exposed rock wall, tearing at him, as though it were a part of the mountain, hating him.

Ten minutes later he was on Agag's Ledge. He rested for a little. Then he unfastened the safety-rope from his waistband and flipped it a couple of times to let Sutherland know. After a moment or two it began to snake upwards. He watched it until it had disappeared above the overhang. Then he sat down carefully on Agag's Ledge with his legs over the side, and felt pleased with himself. Through a rift in the thin mist which now filled the corrie he caught a glimpse of the Lairig Hotel far below.

Sutherland pulled up Callum Lithgow's rope, coiled it carefully and slung it over his shoulders. He passed the safety-rope through the karabiner. There was a hundred and twenty feet of it, which would give him sixty feet of abseil rope and take him comfortably down to Agag's Ledge. He checked the piton, decided that it was satisfactory, and began to rope down.

Duthie was on his feet again and steadied Sutherland as he got to the Ledge. The wind slapped rain at them in gusts.

'Thank you,' said Sutherland.

He began to pull down the safety-rope.

'I see what you mean,' Duthie said.

Sutherland glanced round at him and smiled. Rivulets of rain were running down his face.

'It's an interesting little scramble,' he said. 'Not without its problems.'

'All right. I agree with you. He was lying.'

Sutherland said, 'We'll have to keep moving. The weather's not going to get any better.'

'I still don't think we'll prove anything,' Duthie said.

Sutherland handed him the end of the safety-rope.

'We've a lot of climbing to do yet,' he said. 'It's a long way down. You'll need this.'

Duthie took the end of the rope. He was tempted to say, Me tie a knot? But he changed his mind at the look in Sutherland's eyes, and tied it.

IX

When they got down to the scree an hour later the corrie was filled with thick grey cloud and the rock walls above were shadows, felt rather than seen. The sounds of the corrie were muted and hollow, blanketed by the cloud. The wind was bitterly cold now, and they went into the shelter of a large boulder to unrope. They spent five minutes drinking tea out of a thermos and eating sandwiches. Nothing was said about the Lithgows; prompted by Sutherland, Duthie talked about the climbing he had done in the past; Sutherland talked little and appeared abstracted.

When they had finished, Sutherland began to coil the main climbing rope. He whipped the coil with two or three turns and handed it to Duthie.

'You'd better take this,' he said.

Duthie took the coil and slung it over his shoulders.

Sutherland said, 'That's your route. Down the scree. It'll take you to the lower part of the South-east Buttress, if you keep bearing to the right. Contour round the buttress and you'll come to the path we used on the way up. I should think you'll be below the cloud base. You'll find it easily enough. After that it's plain sailing. You should be at the hotel in an hour. Time to get dried out and have a drink before Keith arrives.'

Duthie heard him out patiently and then said, 'My route?'

'Yes. I've got a hunch that's not the way Callum came down. I'm going his way.'

'I'll come with you.'

'In the circumstances,' said Sutherland, 'one of us must get off this mountain. Intact, so to speak.'

'I don't like the sound of that,' Duthie said.

'I've no intention of breaking my neck. It's merely an elementary precaution.'

Duthie appreciated the validity of his argument. They alone

139

were in possession of information suggesting strongly that a murder had been done. Whether the facts would ever stand up in a court of law was a different matter; but they had to be made known and examined. On the other hand, they – and Sutherland in particular – had done enough.

'It'll be a howling gale before dark,' he said.

'I'll be in before that. I know what I'm doing.'

'I'm sure you do,' said Duthie. 'But we've got what you wanted, haven't we?'

'I didn't want it,' Sutherland said mildly. 'And we haven't got it yet. Not quite.'

'We've got enough, anyhow,' Duthie said. 'Can't we leave the nuts and bolts to the police?'

'It isn't entirely a police matter,' Sutherland said.

For no accountable reason Duthie felt a sudden surge of affection for him; he felt a profound reluctance to leave this no longer young, somewhat incomprehensible man alone in a gloomy, echoing wilderness which could, within an hour or two, turn savage. He wondered afterwards if he had said anything, for Sutherland smiled suddenly and said, 'I'm all right, Alec. Off you go. You can run this scree quite safely. There are no . . . steep places.'

Duthie looked back after he had gone a few yards. Sutherland had already turned and was walking in the opposite direction across the floor of the corrie. He was no more than a shadow in the mist.

'You left him up there?' Christine said. 'Just like that?' There was indignation and disbelief in her face.

There was a good peat fire going in the hearth. Duthie was sitting beside it, unlacing his boots. He had discarded the wettest of his outer clothing, and Keith was arranging his anorak and sweater over the back of a chair at a discreet distance from the heat. Cameron was behind the bar.

Duthie looked up when he had got his laces free and said, 'Yes.'

Christine said, 'Why?'

'That's what he wanted.'

'Couldn't you take any more? I mean he's twenty years older than you are. Surely . . .'

Duthie said, 'I could have hung on for a bit.'

'Then why didn't you? And why didn't he come down with you?'

'Answer yes or no,' said Duthie.

'You know what I mean,' she said furiously. 'It just doesn't make sense.'

'Yes, it does. Up to a point. He wanted to follow what he believed was Callum Lithgow's route from the scree down here to the hotel. He's very thorough.'

'A dram for you, Mr Duthie,' said Cameron, and put a glass on the counter.

'Thanks,' said Duthie. 'I need it.'

He pulled off his boots and padded across to the bar.

'You could have stayed with him,' Christine said.

Duthie picked up his glass, drank and looked at Cameron. Cameron smiled.

'It's the real Glenlivet, Mr Duthie. There's nothing in the world quite like it.'

Duthie looked round at Christine and said, 'He preferred to be alone. And don't worry too much. He knows that mountain.' He took another taste of the Glenlivet and let it lie on his tongue for a moment. And then he said, 'I've got a feeling he's got some kind of personal feud with it.'

'Quite right, Mr Duthie,' said Cameron. 'It killed his wife five years ago.'

Duthie laid down his glass carefully and stared at him. After a moment he said, 'Why didn't he tell me?'

Cameron said quietly, 'I wouldn't think it would be something he would enjoy talking about.'

Duthie looked round at Christine. She met his eyes for a moment, then turned away.

'Did you know?' Duthie asked Keith.

'No, sir,' said Keith. 'I did not.' He looked shocked.

Duthie turned back to Cameron.

'D'you know what happened?' he asked.

'They were climbing together. She was roping down to

Agag's Ledge. And she came off. We never knew why.'

Duthie drained his glass and pushed it across the counter. Cameron refilled it.

Duthie said, 'There was a safety-rope, of course.'

Cameron said, 'Yes. But . . .'

'But she tied it on herself,' said Duthie.

Cameron gave him a startled glance. 'Yes. It's thought she tied it incorrectly. How did you know?'

'Hindsight,' said Duthie. 'I'm very good at it.'

He took his glass and went over to the picture window and stared out at the mountain. The upper two-thirds of it were shrouded in black storm cloud, and tendrils of cloud were reaching down to the lower slopes. It would be dark early tonight, before eight, less than two hours away.

He turned and said to Cameron, 'He thought Callum came down by a different route. And not by the scree.'

'There's no other route that wouldn't mean a big detour,' said Cameron. 'He would come down by the scree all right and over the lower bit of the South-east Buttress.'

'Why?'

'Because he was in a hurry.'

'Was he?'

Cameron looked puzzled. 'Well, of course he was. I think he was hoping Hamish still had a spark of life in him.'

Keith said, 'Would he have come down by the gully?'

'Never!' said Cameron. 'No one would come down by the gully if he was in his right mind. And never if he was in a hurry.'

'What gully?' Duthie asked.

'It's the only other route off the mountain on this side,' Cameron said. 'It goes up into the Coire Dubh, the big corrie where you were.'

'What's wrong with it?'

'It's a drainage line. All the water from the corrie drains into it. It's wet and dirty. Full of rotten rock. There's a big rock fall in there every now and again. No one ever goes into it.'

'I wouldn't bet on that,' Duthie said.

142

He turned and stared out of the window again at the mountain.

The gully was a deep cleft in the side of the mountain below the corrie. All the water from that side of the Bruaich surged down between its steep rock walls in a series of cascades, between deep pools gouged out over the centuries. The rock was not like the rock on the higher parts of the mountain. A scrub of alder and rowan and coarse heather grew in the soil that the rains had washed down from above and deposited in the cracks and crevices. The roots had penetrated deeply, letting in the rain and the frost, and the rock was rotten. It broke away of its own accord or at the touch of a foot. The gully was floored with small broken rock and the vegetable debris that had come down with it.

This, Sutherland thought, had nothing to do with the art of climbing. It was a wet and disagreeable scramble, and if luck held he might get down to the foot of the gully three or four hundred feet below without a broken limb. As he slid and scrambled down from pool to pool he became increasingly aware that he was no longer young. But he was still foolish. Nothing but obstinacy had brought him here. It could have waited. For a better day, for someone else. It was a long time since his anorak had made any pretence of keeping out the weather. He was wet to the skin. And it was cold.

Keith was at the telescope.

Duthie said, 'You won't see a damned thing through that.'

Keith straightened up and looked round at him. There was an edge of hostility between them now.

'Even if he came down by the gully, Mr Duthie, he should have been here within half an hour of yourself. Not much more, anyhow.'

'That depends on what he was doing.'

'What would he be doing in the gully? It's like what Mr Cameron said. Nobody but a nut would go into that place.'

'He didn't tell me what he had in mind,' Duthie said.

Keith turned away, mildly offended, and went over to the bar counter, where he had a half finished drink waiting. Duthie stood at the picture window, looking out at the mountain. The daylight, such as it was, was beginning to go.

Christine had been sitting by the fire, watching Duthie. After a moment or two she rose and went over to him. He looked round at her, said nothing, and looked back at the mountain. The burns on its lower flanks were in spate, and steel grey.

Christine said, 'You're very sure of yourself, aren't you?'

Duthie looked round at her again. She was wrong; but he had sympathy for her, because she was frightened.

'Why didn't you let them go and look for him when they wanted to?' she demanded.

'He wouldn't have thanked them,' Duthie said.

'How do you know? How do you know you're not going to be very sorry about this?'

Duthie said, a little wearily, 'I don't know, Christine. I'm just guessing. But it's an informed guess. I've seen him on that mountain. He can take care of himself.'

'Couldn't the police have gone up tomorrow and done whatever had to be done? It's their job, isn't it?'

'I don't know. I can't tell you. I don't know what had to be done. If anything.' He was silent for a moment; and then he said, 'If you want to know, I think he's been sitting at his desk for five years hating that bloody mountain. And somehow or other he's getting it out of his system.'

She looked at him curiously.

'That's a bit fanciful, isn't it? For you.'

Duthie shrugged.

'I've known him longer than you have,' she said. 'I think it would have to be something a lot more practical.'

'Like what?'

'How should I know?' she said. 'I only type and make the tea.'

Keith had been standing at the bar, watching them across the room. He turned as Cameron came in and went behind the counter and pushed things around a little aimlessly for a moment or two.

'What d'you think, then, Willie?' Cameron said at length.

'You know what I think, Mr Cameron,' Keith said. 'I think it's very curious that the Fiscal hasn't got back before this. I mean, nobody's going to hang around out there on a day like this just for the fun of it. And there's plenty of things can happen to a man even low down on that mountain. You get a kind of wind-chill effect on a day like this. And if he came down by the gully . . .'

'Why would he come down by the gully?' said Cameron. 'He's not that daft.'

'Is there anybody in the back bar?'

'Yes, there's two or three of the boys. They would come out with us.'

'Well, I think it's about time,' said Keith.

Cameron called across the room. 'Mr Duthie!'

Duthie turned from the window.

Cameron said, 'Mr Duthie, we're not prepared to wait any longer.'

Duthie came towards them.

'You and Constable Keith?'

'There's a shepherd and a gillie and one or two others who know the Bruaich in the back bar,' Cameron said. 'They'd come out with us.'

'It's up to you,' said Duthie.

'Will you join us?' Cameron asked.

'No.'

'Alec!' said Christine, in a shocked voice.

Duthie said, 'I've told you what I feel.'

Cameron gave him a hard look and turned and went out.

Keith said, 'I understand, Mr Duthie. You've had a rough day already.'

Duthie thought he detected a slight touch of irony in Keith's voice, and it annoyed him.

'That's got nothing to do with it. Where d'you intend to look?'

'On the scree to begin with. Easy enough to break a leg

there, if you're tired and cold and getting a bit careless.'

'You won't find him there.'

'Well, I don't think he would come down by the gully.'

'Because you don't think Callum Lithgow did?'

Keith began to show some exasperation.

'We've gone into that,' he said. 'Callum was in too much of a hurry.'

'To save his brother's life?'

'Well, hoping to. That's what Mr Cameron thinks. And he was the man on the spot.'

Duthie said, 'He knew damn well Hamish was dead.'

'That's not the impression he gave when he came off the mountain.'

'It's not the impression he meant to give,' Duthie said. 'Because he'd just killed him.'

Keith frowned and looked at Christine, who was staring at Duthie. He looked back at Duthie again and said, 'You mean with the piton coming out?'

'He cut the rope when Hamish was on the way down.'

Keith stared at him. 'But that's murder,' he said, in a voice not much more than a whisper.

'We'll have a job proving it,' said Duthie.

Keith frowned again. 'But the piton came out. It was on the rope.'

'He put it there afterwards.'

'The cunning devil!'

'Shrewd, McKechnie called him.'

'Motive,' said Christine. 'They were brothers. They liked each other, from all accounts.'

'That's another can of beans,' said Duthie. 'We'll open it later.'

Keith said, 'Why would he come down by the gully, Mr Duthie? It seems a daft thing to do.'

'It does, doesn't it?' said Duthie. He thought about it for a moment. Then he said, 'You say nobody ever uses it?'

'Nobody in their right mind.'

'Even a stray tourist?'

'Tourists wouldn't like the look of it. It's rough. And the

climbers give it a miss because the rock's bad.'

Duthie pondered again for a moment, then said, 'So if you happened to drop something there it could lie for a long time?'

'Donkey's years,' said Keith. 'Were you thinking of anything in particular?'

'I've just thought of it,' said Duthie. He crossed over to the fireplace and began to pull on his boots. 'Tell them to wait for me,' he said to Keith.

They were a party of seven: Cameron, Keith and Duthie, and four men from the back bar. They carried a lightweight Thomas stretcher. They went down by the side of the river, now running in full spate; then cut across a peat bog where the white canna danced in the wind and the water in the holes was black. They went up by the side of a rushing torrent that came out of the dark gash of the gully on the hillside above. Mist was thick in the gully, seeping down from the corrie.

They found Sutherland near the foot of the gully. Because of the mist they were within a few yards before they became aware of him. He loomed out of it unexpectedly, sitting like Rodin's Thinker on a rock at the side of a pool, staring down into the water. He was soaked and filthy, and so still that he might have been dead.

Cameron called anxiously, 'Are you all right, Mr Sutherland?'

He had not heard them approach because of the sound of the water. He looked round, raised a hand and called, 'I'm fine.'

As they approached he saw Keith.

'You'll need a grappling iron, constable,' he said. 'Or you might get it out with a long stick. It's only about eight feet deep.'

Keith went to the edge of the pool, balanced on a rock and peered down into the dark water.

'What is it?' he asked.

Duthie said, 'About sixty-five feet of nylon climbing rope. One end roughly cut. The other end palm and needle whipped. Right?'

Sutherland smiled briefly and said, 'Right.'

He heaved himself slowly to his feet. He was chilled to the bone, stiff and very tired. But he made a small negative gesture when Duthie moved towards him, and began to walk down the hill, still putting his feet down solidly. Then he stopped and stared at the stretcher that two of the men from the back bar were carrying.

'What in God's name is that?' he said.

The police were given certain instructions the following morning and later in the afternoon McKechnie came into the office. Duthie took him into Sutherland's room.

'Motive?' asked Sutherland. 'We've plenty of fact and circumstance, very convincing on the face of it. But a motive would be helpful.'

'There was a motive all right,' said McKechnie.

Christine came in with three mugs of tea and the Georgian silver on the tin tray. McKechnie perched on the edge of a hard chair and balanced his mug on his knee. Duthie carried his as he mooched around the room. Sutherland tipped his chair back and said, 'Not a man and his wife and a tertium quid, I hope.'

McKechnie frowned and Duthie said, 'The Fiscal still reads Kipling. He means was Hamish chasing his sister-in-law?'

McKechnie smiled and said, 'No, no, it was nothing like that.'

'Good,' said Sutherland.

'The solicitor for the Ruigh estate is Mr Pringle,' said McKechnie, and Duthie groaned faintly in the background. 'He let me have a sight of old Hector's will. Ruigh was left jointly to Hamish and Callum. Equal shares.'

'Hamish wasn't trying to take over, surely?' Sutherland asked.

'The other way round. He'd taken a sudden notion to go wandering again. He was wanting Callum to buy him out.'

'Would that not have suited Callum well enough?' Duthie asked.

'You would have thought so,' McKechnie said. 'But it wouldn't have suited him at all. It would have ruined him.'

148

'No money,' Sutherland said. 'All in the livestock, presumably.'

'Right. If he'd had to raise a big lump of money, like a third of the value of the estate, which was the sum mentioned, he'd have had to see maybe half his stock go to the sale ring. He'd have been just about back where he started, after all that work and sweat.'

'Couldn't he have borrowed?' Duthie asked. 'Against the stock or the land?'

'Whatever he did in that way,' McKechnie said, 'a part of Ruigh would have belonged to a stranger, to his way of thinking.'

'Yes, I suppose so.'

'Anyhow, they had a big row about it, just the two of them at Ruigh, a few days ago. Hamish was determined to sell, if not to Callum, then to somebody else. And Callum was desperate to keep it in Lithgow hands.'

Sutherland said, 'Highland pride?'

'Call it that if you like. Maybe he was just thinking of his son.'

'He hasn't got one.'

'Mrs Lithgow is two months pregnant,' McKechnie said. 'Callum's convinced it's a son and heir.'

Sutherland stared at him. 'How did you get all this? I hope you didn't get it from Callum.'

McKechnie laughed and said, 'No, no, I have more sense than that, Mr Sutherland. I had a word with herself.'

'Mrs Lithgow? And she was cooperative?'

'She was a bit cagey at first, until I told her what you said.'

Sutherland looked at him uneasily. 'What did I say?'

'That it was done on the spur of the moment. No premeditation. Then she opened up. She was glad to get it off her chest, poor soul. I think she knew it was no accident.'

Sutherland said, 'It's quite possible,' and brooded on it for a moment.

'I hope it was all right to tell her,' McKechnie said.

'It was unwise,' Sutherland said. 'But she's got a rough road to travel. It'll maybe give her some comfort . . . You'd better tell the Chief Inspector. We'll have to gather Callum into the fold.'

'I'll tell him, Mr Sutherland.' He got up and took his empty tea mug out into the main office.

Duthie continued to prowl round the remoter part of the room. Sutherland shuffled a little aimlessly through the papers on his desk.

'I could do with more tea,' he said, looking up. 'This is cold.'

Duthie turned towards the door and said, 'I'll get it.' He paused in the doorway and looked back. Sutherland was busy with his papers again.

'Anyhow, you've beaten it,' Duthie said.

'Beaten what?'

'Your lump of schist and porphyry.'

Sutherland looked up slowly. After a moment he said, 'I haven't the faintest idea what you're talking about.'

'You should read your Bible. First Book of Samuel. Chapter fifteen, verse thirty-two.'

Sutherland looked at him in astonishment. Duthie smiled and went out.

When Christine came in a few minutes later with fresh tea, he was sitting staring at his desk. She laid the mug beside him. He put in one spoonful of sugar and a little milk and stirred it slowly. She was on her way back to the door with one or two signed letters which she had salvaged when he stopped her.

'Is there a Bible in that lot?'

He looked across at the bookshelves.

'I think so.' She went to the bookshelves and found one.

'First Samuel. Chapter fifteen. Verse thirty-two,' he said.

She leafed through the Bible and said, 'I've got it.'

'Read it.'

' "Agag came unto him delicately," ' she read. Then she paused very slightly before she went on, ' "And Agag said, Surely the bitterness of death is past." '

She waited for a moment, watching him. He sat with his hands flat on the desk, staring at nothing. Then he nodded.

'Yes,' he said. 'Thank you.'

She put the Bible away again. As she turned to the door again, Sutherland said, 'He's not to be underestimated.'

'Agag?' she said.

Sutherland smiled at her and said, 'No. Not Agag.'

X

Sutherland decided that he would shoot some of Willie McWhirter's grouse on the Twelfth after all. He was feeling somewhat restored, younger and less jaundiced than he had felt earlier in the summer. The tourist season would shortly draw to a close. The tourists would recede like the tide, leaving a certain amount of garbage of one kind or another, which would be cleared up in due course. It would be possible to get a round of golf again without having to join a queue; to walk in the streets of Glendoran in reasonable comfort and safety; to shop at leisure, without competing with a sweating mass of alien humanity; to get the boat out and do some sailing, if the autumn weather was kind. He had hardly been out in her at all during the summer.

He had said to Duthie a few days ago, 'If you decide to extend your stay in Glendoran, Alec, I'll be glad to write to those concerned and say that I think it's a good idea.'

Duthie was pleased but slightly embarrassed. 'Thanks very much. That's very kind of you,' he said. 'I appreciate it. D'you mind if I take a few days to think it over?'

Sutherland was a little huffed, though he took care not to show it. It had not occurred to him that Duthie might hesitate.

'That's all right,' he said. 'Anyhow, I'm not promising to scatter rose-petals under your feet.'

Sutherland took the late boat over on the afternoon of the eleventh and stayed the night at Glengarve. He was out on the moors early the following day. It was a bright day, pleasantly warm, with a good breeze. McGuffie gave him a butt at the end of the line, which he knew Sutherland preferred. He was not a competitive shot and took no great interest in counting his birds when it was over. If they chose to cross the line somewhere else he was perfectly content to sit back and look at the view, which was splendid from here. His butt was on high ground near the march fence and overlooked the firth and the mountains beyond. He could see the Bruaich; and for the first time in some years he found that he was able to look at it dispassionately and admire it for what it was, a piece of scenery with some good climbing on it. It still, in a curious way, had a personality, but it was no longer the enemy.

It had become evident by mid-morning that Sutherland was going to have a quiet day. Only three or four birds had come within his field of fire, though the guns in the butts farther down the line were banging away busily. His loader, one of McWhirter's gillies, was worried about it; but Sutherland put him at his ease, refused to let him find McGuffie and have him moved to a more active butt; and they sat and smoked and talked and had an occasional nip of Glenlivet out of Sutherland's hip flask and enjoyed the scents of the moor, thyme and heather, peat and warm rock.

Sutherland had noticed the house down in the hollow on the other side of the march fence a little earlier, but it had not connected in his mind. He noticed it again as they were talking.

'Is that Angus McInnes's house?' he asked.

'It is, Mr Sutherland,' said the gillie. He added, 'But Mr McInnes is away just now. You'll know that, of course.'

'Yes, I know,' said Sutherland.

He put down his gun and told the gillie to take any birds that happened to lose their sense of direction and pass this way, and walked down the hill.

He stopped at the march fence. The hollow had an air of great peace. The shingles of the roof and the timber walls had already begun to weather slightly, and were mellow. The bees were at work round the skep. The patches of heather were in full colour, and with the sun out the gorse was in bloom. There was a bright red mooring buoy down below in the little bay. The place had a feeling of waiting, tranquilly, for Angus McInnes to return.

I would give a lot, Sutherland thought, to have a small place like that waiting for me. With a woman in it? He was not so sure about that. But as he considered it, he found that he was more open-minded about it than he would have been only a short time ago. It offered an interesting line of speculation.

He turned and went back up the hill, and saw Willie McWhirter approaching from another direction. They met at the butt.

'I've been looking at your neighbour's place, Willie,' Sutherland said.

'On mature consideration,' McWhirter said, 'I must confess it doesn't look too bad.'

'It's a bit late to have thoughts like that.'

'When does he come up?'

'Thursday, in the High Court.'

'Any idea what will happen to him?'

'None at all.'

McWhirter said, 'I'm damned sorry about it, John.'

'No doubt,' said Sutherland. 'But it wasn't entirely your fault. And I don't suppose you really meant any harm. You can have that as an epitaph, if you like.'

McWhirter smiled wryly and said, 'Thanks very much . . . Lunch at the cars at one o'clock. Does that suit?'

'Fine.'

McWhirter looked at the four grouse lying by the wall of the butt.

'You're not having much luck here. I'll get McGuffie to move you.'

'Don't,' said Sutherland. 'I like it.'

'All right.'

McWhirter was about to turn away, but he paused, looking down at the house.

'Hello,' he said. 'Visitors.'

Sutherland looked. Two men were standing on the patch of gravel in front of the house, talking together. They began to move round the house, examining it. One of them had a piece of paper in his hand.

'Friends of yours?' Sutherland asked.

McWhirter shook his head. 'They're nothing to do with me.'

Sutherland continued to watch them for a moment. In this setting they looked extraordinarily sinister. They were wearing dark lounge suits and bowler hats.

Sutherland walked up the hill to the High Court. It was a typical Edinburgh day, he thought, bright and as cold as charity. He had always found Edinburgh claustrophobic. It seemed overloaded with history and a little self-conscious about it. Glasgow was a warmer city, if dirtier.

The great hall of the High Court was busy. Members of the public hung around aimlessly, waiting, and for the most part apprehensive. Police officers and court officials went quietly about their business. Advocates in gowns and short wigs strolled and chatted.

Agnew saw Sutherland as he came in, and detached himself from a group of other advocates. He was a pleasant, polished, rather rotund man of about Sutherland's age, with humour in his face. He had a file of papers in one hand.

'Hello, John,' he said, as they met. 'Come to watch the massacre of the innocent?'

They shook hands, and Sutherland said, 'If that's what you think he is.'

'I don't,' said Agnew. 'I think he's an old humbug.'

'And you're out to get him?'

Agnew smiled. 'If I can. And within reason . . . I'm puzzled, though.'

'About how it got this far?'

'Yes,' said Agnew. 'I mean, it's not exactly a *cause célèbre*.'

Sutherland said, 'It's largely my fault. I was late for a train.'

Agnew looked at him curiously, but Sutherland said nothing more. Agnew looked at his watch.

'We'd better not complicate the situation by being late for the Judge, too,' he said.

They moved towards the door of the courtroom.

'It's going to be one of these damnable days,' Agnew said. 'It sometimes is with interpreters. The panel and the interpreter will hold long discussions of which nobody else will understand a single word. But the Judge will insist on understanding, quite properly, of course, and he will have prolonged discussions with the interpreter. He's a very meticulous man.'

'Old Melvaig, isn't it?'

'Yes. D'you know him?'

'I've known him for years,' Sutherland said. 'He used to take me fishing when I was a small boy.'

A police constable held open the door for them, and they went inside.

Agnew was wrong. Lord Melvaig gave no trouble at all with the interpreter. He was a long, thin old man with a craggy, weathered face and pale blue far-seeing eyes that would have seemed right in a gamekeeper or a shepherd. He was one of the oldest of the Scottish judges, and he proposed shortly to retire to what had been his boyhood home and spend the last of his days peacefully, fishing. In spite of his years he was still vigorous and alert; and he sat above them, enveloped in the splendour of scarlet and ermine, and pushed the trial along briskly and competently and with no nonsense. He made what both Sutherland and Agnew felt to be an admirable summing up, and sent the jury out.

They came back half an hour later, unable to agree and seeking His Lordship's advice. He gave it to them with great patience and sent them out again. They returned in fifteen minutes and Angus McInnes was found guilty of recklessly discharging a firearm to the danger of the lieges, which was one of the lesser charges on the indictment.

'Well, Mr Agnew,' said His Lordship. 'Do you move for sentence?'

Agnew looked up at the pale blue eyes staring down at him. Six months, suspended, he thought, during which McInnes will sit peacefully on the bench in front of his small house thinking what bloody idiots we are.

'No, my lord,' he said.

'Very well,' said His Lordship, and discharged the panel.

As Angus was turning to leave the dock the Judge leant forward.

'*A MhicAinghais*,' he said.

Angus looked round quickly.

'*Bitheadh seo 'na eiseamplair dhut,*' said His Lordship. '*Na teirig an car an lagh ged a bhitheadh a' bharail bu mhiosa agad air.*'

'*Cha bhitheadh Sin agam Oirbh-se co-dhinbh,*' Angus said courteously.

The Judge smiled and said agreeably, '*Sin thu. Fhalbh dhachaidh a nise 's bi modhail. Agus beannachd leat.*'

'*Beannachd leibh fhein 'ur Morachd,*' said Angus.

'Well, how was I to know the old devil was bilingual?' Agnew said rather plaintively, as they came out into the great hall again.

'You should get acquainted with your judges, my boy,' Sutherland said. 'Get them to take you fishing.'

Agnew looked at him curiously. 'I think you said you were a small boy at the time.'

'Yes. He was born about a couple of miles from my own birthplace. Some years ahead of me, of course. On a croft. Where many of our great men come from.'

'I see.' Agnew brooded for a moment, then said, 'Did you catch what he said?'

'I got the gist of it. It seemed very apt.'

Agnew waited, and then said, 'Yes?'

'Don't fight the Law,' said Sutherland. 'Even when you think it's behaving like an ass.'

'Fair enough,' said Agnew. 'And McInnes?'

'McInnes has considerable style. He said, "I would never think that of Your Lordship."'

Agnew grunted and said a little sourly, 'He should have taken silk. He'd have done well . . . Have you any plans for lunch?'

'I thought of that place where they do haggis and mashed neeps.'

Agnew agreed.

'It's not impossible,' Sutherland remarked, as they went out into the street, 'that these two old gentlemen were sitting looking at each other throughout the trial and thinking, "But for the grace of God there go I." '

Christine was sitting at her desk. It was neat and tidy, a tray with envelopes stamped and ready for the mail, and a tray with two or three letters awaiting Sutherland's signature. She was cleaning the keys of her typewriter, filling in time because the day's work was finished. It had been finished over an hour ago.

Duthie came out of his room.

'What time is it?' he asked.

'Nearly seven.'

'He may not come in, of course. He may go straight back to the flat.'

'He always comes in,' Christine said.

Duthie moved around the room, fiddling. He opened a drawer or two, and closed them again.

'You like him, don't you?' he said suddenly, looking round at her.

'I wouldn't be here if I didn't.'

She began to put away her type cleaning materials.

'He more or less asked me to stay on,' Duthie said.

She fitted the cover carefully over the typewriter before she said, 'Are you going to?'

'I don't know. I told him I'd have to think about it.'

'He needs you. He needs somebody who can stand up to him and talk back. Somebody who can beat him at his own game. Or at least, not be beaten by him. Like you on the Bruaich.'

Duthie thought about it and said, 'I don't know if you're aware of it, but you're being quite complimentary.'

'Yes, I know.'

Duthie grinned. 'It makes a nice change.'

She smiled at him and said, 'Apart from all that, it's nice having you around.'

They heard a car stop outside, then Sutherland's brisk footsteps in the outer hall. The door opened and he came in. He looked at them in mild surprise.

'Not away yet?'

Duthie said, 'We thought we'd wait.'

'That's very considerate of you. Or d'you just want to know what happened?'

'We'd like to know what happened anyhow.'

'He was found guilty of recklessly discharging a firearm to the danger of the lieges. The Advocate Depute didn't move for sentence. And McInnes walked free.'

Christine said, 'Thank goodness!'

'Everything's all right, then,' Duthie said.

'Everything's splendid,' said Sutherland. 'At least, almost everything.'

He went into his room. Duthie looked questioningly at Christine. She gave a small, puzzled shrug. They heard Sutherland moving about, then he came out again. He had left his briefcase and changed his town coat for a heavy shooting jacket.

'I won't be in tomorrow,' he said, as he crossed towards the outer door. 'I'm going to get some fresh air.'

He went out and the door slammed behind him. They heard his footsteps in the hall. Then his car started and pulled away noisily. Duthie looked across the room at Christine.

'Let's go and find ourselves a drink, and then some food.'

Christine nodded and got up from her desk.

Sutherland took his car over in the ferry. On the other side he drove as far as the road could take him, then got out and walked along the track towards Camas Dearg. He was not greatly surprised that the ridge of the roof could not be seen from the track below, and as he came up to the level ground in front of the house his apprehensions were confirmed. There was no ridge, no roof, no house. Its timbers were stacked tidily and only the stone chimney breast was still standing. There was a small mound, covered with a tarpaulin, which he surmised contained furniture and effects.

The collie growled as Sutherland came over the rise.

'*Stad! Bi samhach*,' said Angus, who was sitting on the bench in the middle of the patch of gravel, and the dog lay down again and was silent.

Sutherland came towards him and stopped.

'*Tha latha math ann 'n Aoghnais,*' he said.

Angus said, '*Tha sin ann gu dearbh Mghstr Sutherland.*'

Sutherland said, '*Ni sud a chuis.* I know you have the English.'

Angus stared at him and said nothing.

'You know,' said Sutherland, 'the Advocate Depute is of the opinion that you are an old humbug.'

Angus remained silent for a moment, and then he smiled gently.

'We are all entitled to an opinion, Mr Sutherland,' he said.

Sutherland smiled briefly. He turned and looked at the stacked timber. The place had been meticulously dismembered, almost as though someone had taken pleasure in doing so. But the hollow was still peaceful. It still had the curious air of waiting that he had felt looking down on it from Willie's moor. He looked round.

'Did you do this?'

'It was done while I was away. By the County Council.'

'I'm sorry.'

'It was not your doing, Mr Sutherland. I hold nothing against you.'

'You've nothing to thank me for, all the same. I could have done better.'

He looked round again, at the stack of timber; and he had a sudden, curious impression that it had just been delivered from the timber yard for the building of a house.

'What now?' he asked.

'I will build it again,' said Angus.

'Will you ask for planning permission?'

'I might. And I might not. It's of no great importance.'

'They may come and pull it down again if you don't.'

'Then I will build it again. There is plenty of time.'

He's right, of course, Sutherland thought. It's never too late to start building again. He turned and looked out over the bay with the red mooring buoy, across the firth to the mountains beyond. There was a patch of sunlight on the Bruaich.

'I've asked Mr Duthie to stay on at Glendoran,' he said. 'If he agrees, I might have a bit of time on my hands in the next month or two. If you need any unskilled labour.'

Angus was looking at the view too. After a little he looked up at Sutherland and smiled.

'I would be glad to accept some help,' he said. 'From you, Mr Sutherland.'